FIXIN' TO GET KILLED

"Come on," Tim said under his breath. "Show yourselves, you thieving sonsofbitches."

And then Hell opened up. Rifles were cracking and at least one sixgun was booming. Bullets thudded into the ground and screamed off rocks.

Tim moved only his head, and through the branches of the chokeberry bushes he saw a man standing on the edge of the ravine pointing a rifle in his direction. Knowing he had no chance at all, Tim fired until the hammer fell on an empty chamber.

And all he could think of was that if he'd lived another month he'd be twenty-one.

RUSTLER'S TRAIL
DOYLE TRENT

ZEBRA BOOKS
KENSINGTON PUBLISHING CORP.

ZEBRA BOOKS

are published by

Kensington Publishing Corp.
475 Park Avenue South
New York, NY 10016

First printing: January 1988

Printed in the United States of America

Rustlers' Trail

The shot came from a high rocky ridge off to his right. The sound echoed from a timbered hill back to the ridge.

Timothy Higgins heard the lead slug hit the fork of his saddle before he heard the shot. He bailed off his horse so fast his right spur hooked over the pack horse's lead rope and he fell off. That saved his life. Or the life of his saddle horse.

When he fell, he fell under the horse, something the animal wasn't used to, and it jumped sideways, wheeled and ran back the way they had come, back into the timber. Another bullet screamed off a granite boulder where the horse had been. The pack horse, a gray gelding named Spook, turned around but didn't follow the saddle horse.

Tim stayed down, flat. He crawled to the edge of the sagebrush, away from the creek, where he hoped he wouldn't be a good target. Looking back, he hissed through clenched teeth, "Git. Git out of here, you fool."

Spook had his head up, watching the other horse

5

disappear. "Git," Tim yelled. He took off his hat and threw it at the horse, trying to stampede the animal. It worked.

Spook saw the hat flying at his head, snorted like a freight train, ducked backward, and took off after his buddy.

Now the horses were safe. Tim could only hope he could catch them later. But that wasn't his big worry. His big worry was keeping himself from being shot.

He crawled on his belly, gripping the sixgun in his right hand. Another slug hit the ground two feet from his head. He crawled faster. Another shot. Then he was in a shallow draw, hugging the ground. Still another bullet thudded into a tree across the creek.

The shooter had to be at least four hundred yards away, Tim reckoned. And he had to be up there somewhere near that cathedral-sized boulder. No use even trying to shoot back with the .44 sixgun. With his Winchester he might have a chance. But the rifle was in a boot on the saddle, and the saddle was on a horse that was back in the woods somewhere.

Getting up and going after the horse would be inviting another round from up there. Whoever was shooting would have his sights adjusted now.

He had been expecting it. He knew he was getting closer every day, and he'd been warned that the thieves might have someone watching their back trail. The closer he got, the more likely it was that he would be in some cattle rustler's gunsights.

When he had started after them, he figured they had a good two weeks' lead. But a hundred head of beeves

6

left a trail a blind man could follow, and the thieves could push them only so fast. He'd catch them. And when he did—what? He didn't know what. But catch them he would. Or never go home again.

Old White Shirt Higgins had made that understood. "You either bring them cattle back, or bring back the money for 'em, or you keep right on a-goin'," he'd said.

Tim hadn't answered. He seldom answered. Arguing with his dad was the most useless thing a man could do. It was useless when he was a kid and it was useless now that he was twenty. No use arguing and no use making excuses.

"How the holy humped-up hell could you lose 'em," old White Shirt had bellowed. "How can anybody lose a hundred head of cattle?"

Stub had answered for him. Tried to. Stub was foreman of the HL outfit belonging to John "White Shirt" Higgins, who claimed over 195,000 acres in the valley of the Gunnison River about two hundred miles southwest of Denver.

"There's a terrible lot of country up there," Stub had said. He was only five-four, looking like he'd been sawed off at both ends and his head and feet stuck back on. "And it's rough country. Anybody can steal cattle up there."

Old White Shirt had bristled. His eyes were squinched up and he waved his arms like he was fighting off a swarm of bats. "I don't give a hound dog shit how much country's up there. All he had to do was keep ridin' and keep track of 'em. How the bogged-down hell could he lose 'em. Hell, there's an ocean on both sides of 'em."

Stub had shut up. Foremen came and went on the

7

HL, and Stub had just learned another lesson in how to get along with White Shirt Higgins: say no more than you absolutely had to.

"Well, by God, you'll go find 'em," White Shirt said to his son. "You'll find 'em or you'll roll up your bed and stay off this outfit."

Tim had felt like reminding his dad that he'd left the outfit twice and came back only because the elder Higgins had said he was sick and needed him. Sick, hell. He stood in the middle of the round corral looking like he was strong enough—and mad enough—to bulldog a buffalo. A little pale, maybe, but that was because he'd been staying in the house lately.

Tim had pulled his saddle off a tired dun gelding. He was tired, too. His day had started at first light and now it was after sundown.

He knew the cattle had been stolen. Afternoon thundershowers and at least one hailstorm had wiped out most of the tracks, but it was easy to see where the cattle had crossed Elk Creek in a bunch. He had seen horse tracks, too. It had been mid-September then, and he reckoned the tracks and the droppings had been left there about the end of August. The cattle were prime beeves, fat from a summer of grazing on the tall mountain grass, ready to be rounded up and shipped.

Old White Shirt was stomping around in a circle, waving his arms and cussing with every four-letter word that Tim had ever heard. He was average height, but broad in the shoulders and with a jaw that looked like it was carved out of granite. His son was the same height, but not as broad and with his mother's soft features and dark hair. "Goddamn thieves," White Shirt muttered. "A cowman ain't got a goddamn chance. If the droughts don't drive you to drinkin', the blizzards will. It's always one or the other. And if that don't kill you off, the thieves will. And if you—by workin' your ass to a nubbin—manage to survive all that, the goddamn government'll give the land away. They run the Indians off, then turned the land over to the sodbusters. The goddamn squatters're fencin' off the best water and turnin' the grass upside down, and those goddamn shit-for-brains idiots in Washington say they got a right to do it."

Tim watched the dun roll on the ground and scratch its sweating back. He bent over and unsnapped his leather leggings and turned to go to the bunkhouse. But old White Shirt wasn't through with him.

"I want you on a horse before daylight in the mornin'. Take a pack horse and your bed and whatever groceries you need. But don't take too much. Hell, if you eat too much you'll shit too much, and if you shit too much you won't have any brains left." With that, the boss of the HL outfit stomped off toward the house.

Tim could have told him to go to hell. He sure didn't owe his dad anything. All his life he had been treated worse than any hired man, and the hired men weren't treated too well. Few of them stayed on more than a couple of months at the HL. Tim had slept in the bunkhouse most of his life—except when he was in school at Shiprock—while his dad occupied the big two-story frame house with Old Lady Miggs, his gimpy-legged housekeeper.

There had been talk that he was taking the old lady to his bed, but no one really believed that. She was in her sixties, fat and toothless. Not the kind any man would want to bed down with. Maybe, a cowboy once

9

said during a bunkhouse bull session, that was what made him so cranky: he hadn't had a woman since his wife died. Whatever the reason, John "White Shirt" Higgins, with his walrus moustache, California wool pants, and white shirt, which he wore to set him apart from the hired hands, was one mean sonofabitch to work for. And his son, his only offspring, caught more hell than anyone else.

A good fifteen minutes passed before he dared to raise his head, expecting another shot from up on the ridge. But finally he did raise his head and take a long look. Nothing happened. Where could the rifleman be? There was a pile of boulders as big as a castle near the top, and there were at least three varieties of high country trees covering the side of the ridge. The boulders were the best bet.

Holding his sixgun in both hands, Tim took aim and fired one shot, then ducked. He knew he hadn't hit anyone, but he hoped his shot would draw more fire and give him a clue to the whereabouts of the sniper.

He crawled on his belly a short distance in the draw, raised up, and fired two quick shots. This time he kept his head above the level of the sagebrush, hoping to catch a glimpse of the man. Still nothing happened.

Was he gone? Or was he coming down the ridge to get a closer shot? As long as Tim stayed on his belly in the draw he was safe from any gunman on the ridge, but what if the gunman was coming down? He could be moving Indian fashion, from tree to tree, boulder to boulder. He knew now that Tim was armed only with a pistol, which wasn't accurate at a distance. If he got to the creek he'd be in a position to pick Tim off without even taking careful aim. Tim had to move.

He was no soldier. And although he had been raised on a ranch where nearly everyone, including himself, carried a six shooter, he had never pointed a gun at a human being. He had never been shot at, either, for that matter. Until now. Now someone was trying to kill him.

He reckoned there were five men moving the herd of beeves, and another was watching the trail behind them. That one had seen Tim, knew Tim was following them, and had tried to stop him. He had probably chuckled to himself when he saw only one man on their trail. One against five or six. All the thief had to do was shoot that one man. Or shoot his horses. That would do it. The thieves would be safe.

Stub had volunteered to go along. "Let me take a couple of men and some long guns and go with him," he had said. "One man ain't got much of a chance."

"No, by God," White Shirt had bellowed. "If he ain't man enough to bring back them cattle, then he don't belong on my outfit." They were standing in the biggest corral at daybreak. Tim had wrangled on Turkey, the one saddle mule on the HL. Finding the remuda would have been next to impossible in the dark if it hadn't been for Turkey. The mule knew what his job was, and he could smell the horses. When Tim had led him through the wire gate and mounted, the mule waggled his long ears, hee-hawed a couple of times, then took off at a stiff-legged trot. He went right to the bunch of horses where they were grazing three miles from the

11

ranch buildings.

White Shirt was raving on: "He ain't damn fool enough to ride right up to their camp. What he'll do when he catches up with them is something he's gonna have to figure out for himself. Use his head for once." He added with sarcasm, "If he catches 'em."

Tim had put his saddle on a good bay horse and a crossbuck saddle on the gray named Spook. He placed some groceries, a box of matches, a small iron pot, an iron skillet, a tin plate, and a fork and spoon in the canvas panniers hung on the crossbucks. His canvas-wrapped bedroll went on top of that. A simple squaw hitch held the load down.

Without a word, and with only a couple of cold biscuits and a handful of dried fruit for breakfast, he had mounted the bay, taken the pack horse's lead rope, wrapped it once around the saddle horn, passed the end under his right thigh to hold it, and ridden away.

It had been midmorning when he picked up the trail. He was about fifteen miles from the HL buildings, up in the tall timber where HL cattle grazed in the summer, saving the prairie grasses for winter. Getting there was a steady uphill climb. Then, for five days, he had followed the stolen cattle. The thieves drove them down a long valley between two ridges along a creek. They crossed the top of a high rocky hill where the creek went underground, got down off the hill and into another valley. They were heading east and north.

At times during the five days, Tim swore under his breath at old White Shirt's stubbornness. There were only a few places where cattle rustlers could turn that many beeves into immediate cash. The stockyards at Pueblo was the closest place. Denver was another. Put some men at the stockyards and they'd catch the thieves. Or so it had seemed to Tim.

But not to White Shirt. "Hell, them beeves could be butchered anyplace and the meat sold. Or they could be wintered on somebody's ranch and sold in the spring. Shit, the brands could be worked over and the hair would grow over 'em this winter so they'd look like old brands by next summer. The only way to catch them sonsofbitches is to git on their asses." After thinking it over for five days, Tim had to admit the old man could be right. But he doubted it. The thieves could be heading anywhere, but the packing houses were the best bet. The beeves were fat now. In the spring, after a hard winter, they would weigh less and would bring less on the market. No, whoever stole them would want cash out of them as soon as possible, and nobody bought that much beef on the hoof but the packing houses.

Get after them, old White Shirt had said, and maybe he was right. Someone ought to get after them, camp on their trail. But he hoped his dad had sent some men to watch the marketplaces, too.

So he had camped on their trail, and now he had caught them. Or was close to them. And what was he going to do about it?

Chapter Two

Well, he said to himself, I can't just lie here on my belly. Got to get back across the creek and in the timber. Got to catch my horses. Got to keep after those cattle-stealing sonsofbitches. And—he gulped when he thought about it—got to stay alive.

Crawling with his head down and the sixgun in his right fist, he made his way out of the draw and out of the sagebrush. He was a good target now for anyone who might be watching, and he could feel the hair rising on the back of his neck as he crawled.

Hell, he said to himself, this is a damn-fool thing to do. Anyone with a rifle couldn't miss. Get up and run.

Run, he did. He tried to jump the narrow creek, but landed on the far edge in ankle-deep water, stumbled, got up, and ran. He expected to hear gunfire from somewhere behind him. No, on second thought he wouldn't hear it. Not if it hit him. His leather chaps and heavy spurs slowed him down, but he ran until he was among the pine and out of sight of the ridge across the valley. There, he hit the ground on his belly again and tried to listen.

He was breathing too hard to listen. He held his breath a few seconds, while his ears strained to pick up any sound. Nothing.

Now what? Go look for my horses? No, wait. Wait a few minutes to see if anyone is coming. He hugged the ground and waited, the sixgun in his hand, the hammer back.

Finally, he got up. He was alone. Whoever had shot at him was gone. When the realization came he let out a sigh of relief. Boy, that was close, he said to himself. Got to be more careful. But how the hell do you do that? You either stay on their trail or you give up and go back. Go somewhere. Go to Denver, to my old job in the warehouse. A good safe job. Why in hell hadn't he stayed there? Why in hell had he let the old man talk him into going back to the HL?

"I am sick, boy," the letter had said. "I need you here. If you are any kind of man, you will come home."

Sick, hell. A little pale, but strong as a horse and meaner than a rattlesnake.

But Tim had gone back. He had stayed in the big house for a few days, then moved to the bunkhouse when he couldn't stand the old man's constant grousing.

Shit, he said to himself, as he squatted and took off his spurs, he's right about one thing. I haven't got a brain cell in my head. If I did, I wouldn't be here.

Carrying his chaps over his shoulder and the spurs in his left hand, Tim Higgins walked, looking for his horses. He could see the tracks they'd left in the brown pine needles among the lodgepole pines. They wouldn't stop in the woods, that was for sure. But maybe when they came to a grassy park they'd stop. He walked, watching the ground, hoping he'd find them before dark.

As he walked, he kept looking behind him, watching his own back trail. For five days he'd been alone, the only human in many, many miles, and at times he had felt lonely. Now he thought it would be good to be lonely and not have to worry about who was ahead or behind him. At dusk he found his horses. They had left the woods and drunk at a creek and stopped to crop the tall swamp grass along the creek. The bay, carrying his saddle, didn't want to be caught, but old Spook was glad to see him, smart enough to know that only a human could get that load off his back. Tim tied the gray, and finally managed to get close enough to the bay horse to grab the dragging bridle reins.

Mounted, he rode on up the creek a mile until he came to a spot that was hidden among a grove of aspens with a steep hill on one side and a line of willows on the other. There, he off-saddled and tied each horse by a front foot on a thirty-foot rope. They could graze and lie down to rest.

Supper was cold, a can of tomatoes and a double handful of dried fruit. Tim was afraid to build a fire now. Smoke couldn't be hidden. And to be safe, he unrolled his bed back in the trees away from his horses. He lay on top of it fully dressed until the night air turned cold, and even then he took off only his boots before crawling between the blankets.

For an hour or more he lay awake, his muscles tightening at every sound. They knew he was on their trail and they had to stop him. They had the advantage.

*   *   *

16

The rustlers seemed to know where they were going, but they no doubt had expected a longer headstart. Tim and the other HL cowboys had so much territory to cover that a hundred head of cattle could disappear and not be missed for months. It was by luck that Tim had seen their tracks where they crossed Elk Creek.

Trying to put himself in their place, Tim guessed they were staying in the high hills, thinking they could hide if necessary. Down on the prairie, they wouldn't have a chance if anyone happened to catch up with them.

Let's see, he thought. The railroad had gone as far as the western slopes. They were probably headed for some railroad town. Or, as his dad had said, they could be headed for some homestead in the foothills on the other side of the mountains where the cattle could be wintered, then sold in the spring. Or hell, they could be sold a few at a time to anyone who wanted meat for the winter.

But moving a hundred head of cattle through the mountains might have taken longer than the thieves expected, and that allowed Tim to catch up in five days, or at least to get close. At two places on the trail, he could see where the cattle had got into dense willows, giving the thieves a hard time popping them out into the open again. At other places, the herd had had to be squeezed through narrow canyons and crowded across swift creeks.

Approximately a hundred head. Tim had told the old man he reckoned there were ninety to a hundred missing, and the old man had believed the worst, as usual. It crossed Tim's mind that if by some miracle he did get the beeves back, he'd have to trail them to the nearest shipping point and sell them to the handiest buyer. He couldn't bring them back home by himself.

But that worry only crossed his mind once. *If* he got them back. A mighty big if.

Well, he hadn't spent five days on their trail just to turn around and quit. He'd have to try.

At daylight he cut two thick strips off the slab of bacon he'd brought, fried it, and ate it sitting a hundred feet away from his fire. If the smoke attracted anyone he wanted to see them before they saw him. The bread he'd brought was turning green in spots, and he pinched off the moldy parts and ate a thick slice with the bacon. He wondered when he'd get another decent meal.

Saddled up, he mounted and headed back along the creek where he picked up the trail again. The tracks and droppings told him the herd had gone by two days earlier. He could catch them by midmorning the next day. The spot where the rifleman had lain waiting for him was easy to find. He had waited for hours and smoked five cigarettes. Why, Tim wondered, hadn't he waited until his target got closer where he couldn't miss? If he had waited another ten minutes, Tim would have been close enough that he could have shot the third button off his shirt.

Thinking about that made Tim shiver. By rights he should be dead now with a bullet in his chest. And the thieves should have had two more good horses to add to their collection of stolen livestock.

Now, he was afraid to move. They had tried once and they'd try again. They hadn't stolen cattle and driven them over a hundred or more miles of high hills just to let one man stop them. They were watching for him.

His eyes went over every tree and rock ahead. Nothing moved. Finally, he urged his mount on, leading the pack horse. Now he kept the rifle in his hands and a bullet in the firing chamber. It was useless, he knew. He wouldn't get a chance to use it. The bullet that killed him would come from behind a tree or a boulder, and he wouldn't even hear the shot.

Teeth clenched so tight his jaws ached, afraid to blink, he rode on. Before he headed up each hill, or down each hill, or into each clearing, or around each pile of boulders, he stopped, got down, looked and listened. At the speed he was traveling it would be a couple of days before he caught up with the herd.

Well, better late and alive than never and dead.

At noon he ate more of the moldy bread, carefully pinching off the green spots, and a handful of dried fruit. An hour before sundown he stopped and made his camp in thick timber, believing that whoever was watching the thieves' back trail would expect him to keep coming until dusk.

When he crawled between his blankets, two hundred yards away from his saddles and panniers, his stomach reminded him that he'd eaten too little and he needed a hot, solid meal. To hell with it, he said under his breath, unless I'm lucky I'll never eat another good meal.

It was the magpie that woke him up. Two of them were fussing over his camp, picking up the pieces of green bread he had left on the ground. The big black and white birds preferred to eat dead flesh, but they'd eat most anything else that was available. The sun wasn't up yet, but there was a high ridge to the east, and Tim reckoned the sun came up late at that spot. The high-altitude air was cold, and he shivered as he built a small fire, put the skillet on to heat.

When he mounted and rode away, he couldn't help noticing what a clear blue the sky was and how clean and cool the air was. The grass was green and the wild flowers were every color imaginable. Fall was the best time of the year in the mountains. It was between the rain and hail of summer and the deep snow of winter.

A beautiful day.

He was gaining, but not as fast as he expected to. Being careful took time. At the top of a high ridge, he got off his horse, lay on the ground, and studied the country ahead. More ridges and hills, with a narrow creek winding like a snake track at the bottom of the ridge. Green willows lined the creek in most places. Off to his right a marmot poked its head up among some rocks and chirped. It sat straight up on its hind end, chirped again, jerked its tail, and ducked down into its hole.

Whistle pigs, the cowboys called them.

Suddenly, Tim's eyes narrowed. Smoke. Far ahead. It was them. No, it couldn't be. Not in the middle of the day. But someone was down there. Four miles? Approximately. Who?

He mounted and rode downhill, keeping his eyes busy and his ears straining.

The thieves had pushed the stolen herd straight down the hill, and Tim could see where some of the cattle and horses had slid on their hind feet. At the bottom he followed the tracks around a rocky hill into the mouth of a narrow valley covered with sagebrush and boulders the size of a bushel basket. Traveling was easy for a few miles, then the valley ended and the herd had had to be urged uphill again to the top of another ridge. From there, they had followed the spine of the ridge, then dropped down into another sagebrush valley.

That was where he saw the cabin.

At first he saw only a two-room log cabin with a dirt roof, but when he rounded a pile of boulders a small shed came into view and a long, three-sided stock shelter and some corrals. All were made of tree trunks. A spotted milk cow with a heavy bag and long tits grazed near the stock shelter, and a team of sorrel horses with the harness on stood in the corral, eating out of nose bags.

Tim had to get down and open a wire gate, then he rode across a two-acre field that had recently been plowed up. Dirt-packed potatoes littered the ground. A farm crop. Harvesttime. Kind of puny-looking spuds.

Smoke came from a stone chimney on one end of the cabin, but no numan was in sight. Tim rode closer. Stopped suddenly.

A canvas-wrapped form hung from a rafter of the stock shelter. Blood had soaked through the canvas. A freshly killed beef. Had to be. The canvas wrap would keep it fresh for days, maybe even weeks, depending on the weather. After a week of summer temperatures, a man would have to take a good long sniff of the meat before he cut off a piece for supper.

The stolen herd had gone within two hundred yards of the cabin, and the fresh meat had been an HL steer.

Tim turned his horse and went back to the trail,

21

followed it a short distance, reckoned the herd had gone by sometime the day before, then turned back to the cabin. He stopped in front of the door and sat there a moment on his horse. Then he yelled, "Hello."

The plank door opened and a man came out. He wore bib overalls, lace-up high-top shoes, a blue shirt with the sleeves rolled up, and he carried a double-barreled shotgun. "Whatta you want?" His voice was far from friendly.

Chapter Three

Tim stammered, "I, uh, I'm looking for a stolen herd of cattle."

The shotgun was hanging in the crook of the man's left arm and pointed at the ground. It could be brought up and aimed at Tim's chest in a split second. And if it was loaded with buckshot it wouldn't have to be aimed.

"Ain't seen no cattle."

Tim looked back at the stock shelter. "Is that beef?"

"Yeah. We butchered the milk cow's calf."

Tim stayed on his horse. It would have been bad manners to get down without being invited to. It was also bad manners not to invite him to get down. A small girl, no more than three, barefoot and wearing a dirty white dress, came out of the cabin. The man turned his head and looked back at her.

"Git back in the house."

The little girl ran back inside.

"The herd of cattle I'm looking for crossed the creek right over there." Tim pointed at the spot two hundred yards in front of the cabin. "And it wasn't long ago."

The man said nothing, only looked hard at Tim.

"About the time that beef was killed."

"I told you what we got there."

They stared at each other, neither making a move. The door behind the man opened again and the little girl and a boy, older than the girl, looked out but stayed inside. He was lying, Tim knew. Lying like hell. But what could he do about it? He decided to try a bluff.

"Where's the hide?"

"Berried it."

"You buried it? Why? It would have made good leather."

"Didn't have time to tan it and didn't want it stinkin' up the place."

"Was it branded with an HL?"

"Naw."

"Want me to go fetch the sheriff? He'll make sure you dig it up and show it to him."

The farmer's face muscles twitched, and for a second, Tim thought he was going to bring the gun up. They continued staring at each other, still not moving.

Fetch the sheriff, hell. He didn't know where the nearest sheriff was. Didn't even know where the nearest town was. He'd have to leave it be and go on. Without the hide he couldn't prove the beef belonged to the HL, and he wasn't about to try to dig up the hide. Not even if he knew where it was buried. Stealing beef from the big cow outfits was common practice. Nesters like this one did it all the time. They had to be caught with the hide to be arrested, and when they were arrested trial juries usually found them innocent. Why, the jurors asked themselves, would anyone who owned several thousand head of cattle want to prosecute a poor farmer who stole one to feed his family?

It was getting so the farmers outnumbered the cattlemen.

But dammit, Tim couldn't just turn his back to it, either. He went on with his bluff. "All right, I'll get the law. We'll see whose beef you killed." He reined the bay toward the creek and the cattle trail.

"Wait a minute."

Tim stopped, looked back.

"I bought it from some fellers that was drivin' a herd of cattle through here."

"When?"

"Yestiddy."

"Were they branded with an HL?"

"Yeah, I b'lieve they was. They said they was takin' 'em to the railroad over to Rosebud and was gonna ship 'em to Denver."

With a flick of the reins, Tim turned the bay horse back and stopped in front of the man. "They were stolen from the HL outfit in Parker County. I've been on their trail for six days. No, seven days."

"You by yourself?"

"Yeah."

"What you gonna do when you ketch 'em?"

"Sic the law on them."

"I didn't steal nothin'. I paid 'em forty dollars for that steer."

"How much?" Tim knew he was lying again. Hell, he didn't have forty dollars. Hell, his whole potato crop wouldn't bring forty dollars. Farmers like him came and went. They arrived in the summer, saw the good green grass and allowed this was the place to plant

25

some corn, melons, spuds, or something. What they didn't know was the growing season was so short nothing planted by man had a chance to grow to full size. Like those potatoes over there. They'd help feed a family through the winter, but they couldn't compete on the market for spuds grown in better climates.

Most of the farmers gave up and moved on, looking for the Promised Land. What they left behind was the ruins of shacks, plowed-up ground where weeds grew instead of grass, and a tangled mess of barbed wire. Yep, the man was lying. But what could Tim do about it?

"How many men were with the herd?"

"Six."

"Was any of them hanging back, looking behind them?"

"Yeah, there was one that came along after the rest of 'em left."

"How far is Rosebud?"

"You don't know?"

"You say the railroad goes through there?"

"Yeah."

"And are there stock pens, a place to load cattle?"

"Shore is."

"How far?"

"About twenty mile." The farmer squinted at him. "You don't know this territory, do you?"

"Can't say I do."

"You belong to the HL?"

"My dad owns it."

"How come you're trailin' a bunch of cattle rustlers by yourself?"

Not knowing how to answer, Tim hesitated, then grinned a lopsided grin. "Because I'm crazy."

The farmer stared at him, unbelieving, then a grin split his face, too. "You must be."

For a few seconds they grinned at each other, then, "When did you eat last?"

"This morning."

"We was just havin' some dinner. Git down and come in. The old woman'll put another plate on the table."

Tim dismounted and stretched his legs. "Mind if I unload this pack horse? He needs to rest his back."

"Naw. Put 'em in that pen over there. I'd let you have some feed for 'em, but we ain't got enough to git our own stock through the winter."

"They can get plenty to eat when I camp for the night."

There were two kids in the cabin and a woman. The woman was thin, with arms and legs that looked like strips of rawhide, and stringy brown hair that hung down to her shoulders. Her cotton print dress was shapeless. And she was pregnant. Tim guessed she was within a month of calving. When she smiled she showed a gap in her front upper teeth.

"We're proud to have you, Mr. Higgins," she said after Tim introduced himself. "Set down. We've got some roast ribs of beef that we butchered yesterday and some of our own-grown potatoes and carrots."

The room was sparsely furnished, with a two-burner cook stove, a table made of rough two-inch lumber, aspen trunks for legs, and chairs made of the same materials. An open cupboard containing a bag of flour, a bag of sugar, and canned goods was nailed to the log wall.

"I sure do appreciate this," Tim said. "I haven't had a

good meal for six days now. Or seven. Seems like I've lost track of time." He was also glad to have someone to talk to.

The boy looked to be about ten years old, sun-bleached hair, baggy overalls, bare feet. Eyes as big as saucers as he took in Tim's chaps and spurs.

"Howdy," Tim said. "My name's Tim. What's yours?"

"Arthur." The boy mumbled the name.

"Arthur. That's a fine name. There was a king named Arthur once. You read about him?"

The woman answered. "I taught 'im to read and write some, but we ain't got any books for him to practice on."

"We got a big book with a lot of pitchers in it," the boy said.

"He's talkin' about the Montgomery Ward catalog," the woman put in. "He's learned to read some of the words but not all of them."

"You keep working at it, son. You'll be glad you did."

Silently, Tim was glad he'd had the opportunity to go to school. That was one thing old White Shirt had insisted on. Tim had stayed with an elderly couple named Jennings in Shiprock and attended the two-room school there. On weekends and in the summers he'd stayed at the ranch. Most of the time in the bunkhouse. He was sorry for anyone who couldn't read.

The farmer and his family bowed their heads while the farmer mumbled grace, and Tim bowed his head, too. Then the roast ribs, mashed potatoes, and water gravy was passed around, and it was all good.

He waited until after the meal, when he and the farmer were outside, before asking about the thieves. "You say there were six?"

"Countin' the one that was stayin' behind."

"Did you recognize any of them?"

"Naw. Never seen 'em before."

"What did they look like? I mean, were they fat or skinny, tall or short?"

"Nothin' peculiar about about any of 'em, 'cept the one with a hook where his left hand ought to be."

"A hook?"

"Yeah. Feller lost his hand somehow."

"Was he kind of thin, about average height, with light-colored hair?"

The farmer rubbed his jaw. "Yeah, that fits 'im pretty good. Know 'im?"

"Yeah," Tim said sadly. "I know him."

"How'd he lose his hand?"

"In a blizzard. It froze."

"Oh. It don't seem to bother 'im much."

"No. He's learned to do as much with one hand as most men can with two. Uh, was there anybody else that you could describe?"

"Wal, there was a boy. 'Bout fifteen. Not old enough to shave, anyways. Didn't talk."

"Hmm." Tim looked down at his boots. "Well, I'd better get going. How far did you say the town of Rosebud is?"

" 'Bout twenty mile. You ought to git there about the same time as them cattle. They said they was gonna foller our wagon tracks to Rosebud."

29

"Yeah. Well, thanks for the dinner. Sure was good."

"You're welcome. Say, you ain't gonna tell the sheriff 'bout that beef, are you?"

"Naw. You didn't steal it." Tim grinned. "Not with six armed men guarding it. Or was it five men and a boy?"

He loaded his pack horse and tightened the cinch on his saddle. The tow-headed boy watched him, eyes wide.

"Is that a real cow pony?"

"Yep. A good one, too. Gets to hunting boogers sometimes, but he's not hard to handle."

"Huh?"

"You know, gets to looking for something to booger at."

"Oh. I'm gonna be a cowboy when I git big enough."

Tim put his foot in the stirrup and swung into the saddle. "I'm not so sure that's a good idea, son." He wrapped the pack horse's lead rope around the saddle horn. "The work's hard and the pay is nothing to brag about."

"Oh."

"Find yourself a good place to farm and stick with it. The world has to eat something besides beef."

The boy said nothing for a few seconds, then, "I'm gonna git me some boots and spurs when I git big enough."

Tim grinned. "Seems like when a kid gets it into his head to be a cowboy he's gonna try it no matter what anyone says." He touched the bay's sides with the spurs and rode away. When he crossed the creek he looked back. The whole family was watching him. He waved. They waved.

Too bad about them, he said to himself as he picked up the cattle trail. Nice, God-fearing folks. Hope they find a good spot to settle on soon. The thieves probably gave them a steer for a woman-cooked meal and some groceries. Hell, they could afford to give a steer away. It was stolen anyhow.

Chapter Four

It was danger time again. The herd had passed through here a day earlier. He was close. And, as he had already known, one of the thieves was hanging back, looking for him. He followed the trail into a stand of aspen, then into pine and spruce, and tried to think like a thief.

Let's see. If I was watching my back trail for pursuers I'd get up on a ridge or a hill and lie on my belly. Or wait among the trees on the other side of a park. Wait for the pursuers to ride into the park where they'd be good targets. I'd keep my horse out of sight but not too far away. Might have to catch him quick and ride. Tim saw a clearing ahead and reined up.

He could be right over there behind those rocks. If I ride into that park I'm a damned fool. He dismounted, hoping he'd be harder to spot afoot. Eyes and ears straining, he studied the clearing and trees and boulders on the other side of it. Nothing moved.

Well hell, he mused. I don't have to ride out into the open. He mounted again. I'll just go around it. He

32

reined his horse to the left, staying back in the trees, looking for a way to get around the park. A half mile farther he came to a steep timbered hill. He reined up and calculated it would take most of an hour to ride to the top of that hill, and then he'd be so far away from the cattle trail it would probably take another hour to find it again.

Tim decided to cross the park right there, hoping he was far enough away from the rifleman—if there was one watching the park—that he wouldn't be seen. Once that was decided, he crossed a stream that was barely a trickle, but which created boggy ground on each side, ground where the grass grew green and high. The horses had to work hard, put their heads down and buck their way through the belly-deep bog, and Tim felt sorry for old Spook. The pack horse was carrying a dead weight with tight cinches.

Out of the bog now, he urged his horses into a lope and got across the clearing and into the trees as fast as he could. There were no gunshots, but still he couldn't be sure he wasn't seen.

It was something to think about. If he was seen, the rifleman would hurry to the next good ambush spot and wait for him there. But what if he wasn't seen?

Could he come up behind the man?

He held his horses still for a few minutes, letting them blow while he thought it over. If he could get behind the man, get the drop on him, he would eliminate some of the danger. How? Shoot him? He'd have to. Or could he disarm him and take him to the town of Rosebud and turn him over to the sheriff? Naw, that wouldn't work. The cattle were following the wagon road to Rosebud and he'd have to stay behind them. And he'd have to keep the man prisoner all night.

Damn. He wished he knew the country. There had to be other ways to get to town. If he knew the country maybe he could go around the thieves and the cattle and get there ahead of them, have the sheriff watching for them. Then when they came to the stockyards, he'd be ready to read the brands and arrest them.

But after looking up at the hills and rocky cliffs and tall trees, Tim knew that if he didn't follow the trail and the wagon tracks he could climb a lot of mountains before he got anywhere. He had to stay on the trail.

All right, he said to himself, the thing to do was try to get behind the man who was watching the back trail. Get the drop on him. Then if he wanted to make a fight of it, they'd just have to, by God, fight. If he had to shoot somebody, so be it. Hell, somebody was trying to shoot *him*.

If there was actually a man there.

Riding on, Tim cut a wide route around the clearing until he reckoned he was north of it, between it and the trail. Dismounting, he tied his horses to an aspen, took off his chaps and spurs and left them on the ground, then walked. Carrying his Winchester with a cartridge in the firing chamber and the hammer back, he walked, trying to make no sound. Soon he realized he had miscalculated, that the park was farther away than he had thought. He walked on, hurrying from tree to tree, boulder to boulder. Stopping behind each tree to look and listen.

It was a horse he saw first. Tied to a tree. The horse heard him and looked in his direction. Damn, he hoped the man wouldn't look in the direction the horse was looking. Wherever he was. Couldn't be far away, but where?

Moving slowly, carefully, like a hunter stalking elk, Tim worked his way back toward the park. The man had to be between the horse and the park. Just waiting there for a shot at whoever was following the stolen herd.

Tim stood behind a big spruce with branches that reached the ground and took a long look at the country ahead of him.

He saw the man the same instant the man saw him.

A rifle cracked. The explosion echoed among the hills. Splinters flew off the tree close to Tim's head. Tim ducked back.

For a moment he stood there, afraid to move. The bullet had grazed the tree only inches from his face. He had come within inches of being killed. Now his heart was pounding and his pulse was racing. Only inches. He stood petrified with fear. Move away from the tree and a bullet would plow into him and end his life. Stand there too long and a bullet would plow into him. Got to move. Find the man. Shoot. Damn. The man knew where Tim was, and now Tim didn't know where the man was. Fear had him in its grip and he stood there shaking with it.

Footsteps. He was coming. Got to do something. Got to move. Move, dammit.

Without even looking to see where he was firing, Tim poked the rifle barrel around the trees and squeezed the trigger. The boom of the gun bounced back from a cliff on the west. Then there was silence.

Had he hit him? Naw. Tim knew he hadn't hit anyone. He was no better off than before he'd fired. His enemy had him trapped behind a tree. Trapped because he was afraid to move. Dammit, he had to move.

Eyes wild and brain whirling, Tim looked around. To his left was a short, low string of granite boulders. If he could get behind those rocks he'd have a better fort than the tree. If. Another big if. That sonofabitch probably had him in his gunsights now. Move and be shot.

Hell, move *or* be shot.

Old White Shirt was right. His son took after Mrs. Higgins. A lady. Gentle and kind. Wouldn't hurt a fly. Damned kid didn't have what it takes to be a cowman. Ought to be milking cows on some squatter farm. Standing there behind that tree shaking in his boots while a cattle thief walks up and puts a bullet in him.

Footsteps again. The man was angling to his right, trying to get in a position where he couldn't miss. Running.

Running? Hell, if he's running he can't be taking aim. Not good aim. Move. Now. Move, dammit.

Bending low, Tim ran for the boulders. A bullet hit the ground near his left foot, another pulled at the side of his shirt. He hit the ground facedown, sliding behind the boulders. Another bullet spanged off a rock.

For a few seconds he couldn't believe he'd made it. He was safe. The rocks made a good fort. The sonofabitch couldn't shoot him now.

Or could he? Of course, he could. He was no better off here than he was behind that tree. Well, yes, he was. Now he could move a short distance without exposing himself. The shooter knew he was behind a string of boulders, but he didn't know exactly where behind the boulders.

Crawling on his hands and knees, Tim clutched the Winchester and moved to a different spot five yards away. He jacked the lever down on the rifle and saw the mechanism shove another .44 cartridge into the barrel. What now? Shoot, that's what.

But if he looked over the rocks he'd be seen and he'd be a target again. Have to look. Can't just lie here.

His face and hands were skinned from hitting the ground facedown, but he hardly noticed that. Carefully, he got to his knees and peered over the edge of a hunk of granite. He saw nothing, and in three seconds he ducked again. There was silence. Waiting about fifteen seconds, Tim raised his head a second time. Now he took a long look. Then he heard hoofbeats. The man was leaving.

With a sigh, he stood and looked in the direction the horse and rider had gone. His hands were still trembling as he let the hammer down on the Winchester. Damn, he wasn't cut out to be a gunfighter. He didn't have the nerves for it.

He started walking toward his horses, and a horrifying thought came to him. What if the thief found his horses and made off with them? He'd be afoot a long way from nowhere. And he'd be laughed at if he ever went back to the HL.

Running now, stumbling over the rocks, not trying to be quiet, he headed in the direction he'd come from. He saw his horses, and he saw the man again. The man was getting down from his mount, no doubt planning to untie old Spook and the bay and lead them away.

No you don't, Tim muttered. No, by God, you don't. He stopped, threw the rifle to his shoulder, took a quick glance down the barrel and squeezed the trigger.

Again, the sound bounced from hill to hill. The man ahead jumped as if he'd been kicked in the seat and ran around to the off side of his horse. Tim fired again, aiming for the man's legs, but hitting the ground under the horse.

The horse, a good-looking sorrel, didn't like the sound of a bullet hitting the ground under its feet, and it went straight up, kicked back with both heels, and tried to jerk away from the man.

Tim got a good look at him then. He was short, thick, with a dark beard and a high-crown black hat. No one he had ever seen before. The man was in a predicament. He could let go of the horse and shoot back or he could hang on to the horse. He chose to hang on to the horse, and managed to get his foot in the stirrup and get mounted. He was a cowboy. Only a cowboy could mount a plunging horse and hang on to a rifle at the same time. But he couldn't aim a rifle with one hand, and he gouged his spurs into the animal's sides and rode away at a dead run. Hooves clattered over the rocks.

Tim took aim. He had the man's back in his sights, his finger on the trigger. Shoot, his mind told him. He tried to kill you. Shoot the sonofabitch. His finger tightened. Then the man was gone. Into the trees and out of sight.

For a long moment, Tim stood there, still holding the rifle in a firing position. Finally, he lowered the gun, cursing himself. You should have done it. Why the hell didn't you shoot? Old White Shirt was right, you're a pantywaist. Just like your mother. Let some sonofabitching thief come within a hair of killing you, and when you get a chance to kill him you just stand there.

He dropped to the ground and sat cross-legged, holding the rifle across his knees and his chin in his hands. I've got no business here, he told himself. Why don't I just quit? Take off across country, follow a game trail, an Indian trail or anything, and come out of the mountains somewhere far away from any stolen cattle. Go back to Denver. Get another job in the city. Do anything but try to shoot it out with six thieves who wouldn't hesitate one second to put a bullet in my back. I'm no cowman and never will be. That was what White Shirt said. Often.

For a long while he sat on the ground, then stood up slowly and went to his horses. He'd go on. Do the best he could. One day his horses would be found and someone would follow the cattle trail back and find his body. At least old White Shirt would know he'd tried. Shit. He shook his head sadly.

If he lived another month, he'd be twenty-one.

Chapter Five

Caution was keeping him away from the herd, away back. But he reckoned he really didn't have to catch up yet. Just so he got to Rosebud before the cattle were loaded on rail cars and shipped out. That was all he had to do, really. He'd heard enough about the railroads to know that cattle cars were seldom available when a cattleman needed them. The herd wouldn't be leaving Rosebud right away. He could afford to stay back, take his time, and play it safe.

Safe? Not by a long shot. But maybe his enemies wouldn't look for him this far back. At midafternoon he made his camp. The horses needed time to graze and rest. He picked a grassy park to stake his horses in, but he unrolled his bed and fried his bacon back in the trees where he wouldn't be so easy to see. This could be his last day of camping out on a cattle trail. Tomorrow, if the farmer had been right, he ought to see the town of Rosebud. Tomorrow night he'd sleep on a soft bed in a hotel. He'd take a hot bath and eat a woman-cooked meal again.

The danger would still be with him, but it wouldn't be so intense. When the thieves saw him ride into town, they'd know he was the one on their trail and they'd try to shut him up. He'd have to be careful, stay among people, try to get to the sheriff first thing.

Tim slept with his sixgun under the blankets with him and his rifle beside the bedroll. Twice during the night he woke up, thinking he'd heard something. Someone sneaking up on him. Both times he lay awake for an hour or more, listening, fear gripping him. He'd slept on the ground many times in his life, and most of the time he didn't mind it, even liked it. But tonight every mouse rustling through the pine needles caused his heart to beat faster. Daylight was a relief.

He rolled out, pulled on his boots, and went to his horses, stopping first among the trees and taking a long look around. The horses were busy cropping the mountain grass. Breakfast was more of the bacon, a can of hominy, and a handful of dried fruit. He was out of coffee and the bacon was beginning to smell suspicious.

The horses drank their fill in a nearby stream—snow runoff from somewhere near the Continental Divide—and he washed his face in the same stream. Saddled up and mounted, he went back to the cattle trail and began another day of trying to do what old White Shirt had sent him to do. He rode slowly, looking ahead, trying to catch movement, afraid he'd see movement.

The trail wound between the high hills and went over the low ones. Most of the way it followed a stream, but at places the stream went between narrow gaps in the hills and boulders where a wagon—and a herd of cattle—couldn't travel.

Before he topped each hill he stopped, got down, and crawled on his hands and knees to the top. He went on only after studying everything in front of him. When the sun reached its highest point, he off-saddled and staked his horses, letting them graze and rest for an hour while he ate another can of beans and more dried fruit. He reckoned it was shortly after noon when he saddled up again and went on. An hour later he topped a hill, looked down on a wide valley, and saw the river.

He saw the cattle, too.

The river had to be the Gunnison or the Colorado, he didn't know which. It snaked its way through the valley, running west to east, telling Tim he was on the east side of the Continental Divide. From where he sat, he could see that the river was narrow and swift in places and wide and gentle in other places. It came out of a canyon about two miles west and was running down the valley and into the tree-studded hills on the east. The cattle were across the river and about two miles beyond it. They were moving.

Tim guessed that the cattle had crossed the river somewhere below him and the crossing had slowed them down. They wouldn't reach Rosebud that day. He guessed too that every man was needed to push the herd into the water and get it across. Tim had swum cattle across the Gunnison and he knew what a job that could be.

The best way, he had come to believe, was to cut out about a dozen and crowd them into the water, get them across, and hold them on the far bank dripping and bawling. That made it easier to get the rest of the herd into the water. Two riders stayed on point in the water to keep the leaders moving in the right direction, and other cowboys kept them from turning back. It could be dangerous.

Two years before, Tim and five HL riders had had to swim about a hundred and fifty head across the Gunnison, and it had almost turned into a tragedy. The river was deep and swift, but the cowboys knew what they were doing and it had been going fairly well until the leaders got to the middle. Then a fallen tree had come floating downstream right in front of them, and the leaders had tried to turn back. The result was a milling, floundering mass of cattle.

The cowboys knew they had to get them moving again, get them strung out, or they would drown. Yelling like Texas Comanches, they had spurred and plow-lined their horses into the milling mass, slapping at cattle with coils of catch ropes, their hats, or anything they could find. Though only eighteen, Tim had done his part. He'd urged his mount into the middle of the mess of heads, ears, and horns, and beaten at the cattle with his rope, screaming his head off. His horse had rolled over in the water, and Tim lost his seat. Grabbing at a cow's horns, he'd held on, still screaming and kicking. He kicked the cow in the side, slapped her in the face, and got her turned toward the far bank. Finally, the milling broke, and the cattle were moving forward. When Tim saw that his cow was heading in the right direction, he had let go of her horns and grabbed her tail and let her pull him, coughing and wheezing, out of the water.

He had felt miserable until someone commented, "Lost one, but I think that's all. We saved 'em, boys." Tim's horse had come out a hundred yards downstream, and the cowboy who caught him and led him up said,

"You're a good hand, Timothy, my boy."

Now, as Tim looked across the river somewhere near the center of Colorado, he figured this crossing would be easy.

But what was puzzling was how a wagon could cross the river. The thieves had been following wagon tracks until they came to the river, then lost the tracks somewhere. Or deliberately left them. One thing was certain, if the farmer could get to town in his wagon, there had to be a better place to cross the river.

Maybe there was a bridge somewhere, a plank bridge that wouldn't hold up under the hooves of a hundred head of cattle, but Tim had taken a long look from up on the hill and he hadn't seen any. The thing to do, he decided, was to go back to wherever the cattle had left the wagon tracks and follow the wagon tracks to town. But on second thought, maybe the railroad pens were not in the town. The railroad built some of its stock pens far away from town, out in the open where cattle could graze until cattle cars were available.

Or maybe the pens were in town, but the thieves planned to graze the cattle out of town for a time. Or . . . ?

Well, he would follow the cattle. At least far enough to see where they were going. Stay back but watch, then go for the law.

Touching spurs to the bay, Tim sent him down the hill, scattering small rocks. The pack horse followed without letting the slack come out of the lead rope. At the bottom of the hill, he followed the trail north across the sagebrush valley to the river. There, the cattle had milled. He could see that by the tracks. The rustlers had held them in a bunch while someone went on down the

44

river looking for a better place to cross. Tim followed the tracks to a spot where it would be easier to crowd a herd of cattle into the water. Out toward the middle, the river looked deep. Over a horse's head. They'd had to swim.

He dismounted and loosened the cinches. A horse couldn't swim with a tight cinch. His bed, groceries, everything would get wet, but maybe he'd get to the town before night. Using his spurs when necessary, he urged the bay up to the water. The horse snorted and tried to turn back, but obeyed the rein. When it got its front feet in the water, Tim had to use the spurs even more. "Come on, old feller, you can swim. It won't hurt you to get wet." Now the pack horse was pulling back. "Come on, dammit. Shit." He reined his mount back onto the bank and pulled the pack horse's head up to his right knee, wrapped the lead rope around the saddle horn twice, held it. "All right, let's go."

The bay stepped into the water, stopped, took another step. Old Spook was right beside him and was in the water, too. Gigging the saddle horse now, Tim got the horses in the cold water up to their bellies, then up to his knees. The water was moving faster out toward the middle, but not too fast. They could swim it. Then a terrifying thought came into Tim's head.

Out there in the water, swimming, they were a perfect target for anyone who wanted to shoot them.

Chapter Six

There was nothing Tim Higgins could do about it. He had to cross the river. With fear in his throat, he stayed in the saddle until his horse's feet could no longer reach the bottom, then he allowed the water to lift him off. He wrapped the reins once around the saddle horn and hung on to the saddle, wishing he'd taken off his spurs and chaps. Swimming was impossible with all that on, and he had to depend on the swimming ability of his horse to keep from drowning.

He could feel his boots filling with water, and the left one started to come off. Tim reached down and pulled it back up. "Where the hell is the bank," he muttered. "Come on, old ponies." Horses were good swimmers when they weren't encumbered, and the saddle horse was having no trouble. But the pack horse, carrying a dead weight, was floundering. "Come on, Spook. Keep your head up, old boy."

Tim took the pack horse's lead rope and tied it to the saddle horn. "Now it's up to you, feller," he said to the

46

bay. "Keep those feet paddling."

Once, his head went under and he got a mouthful of water. Gasping and sputtering, he hung on to the saddle with one hand and paddled with the other. Then the bay's feet touched the bottom, and then its back was above water. "Pull, old feller," Tim pleaded. "Got to pull your partner out." The bay pulled and then the pack horse's back was above water. In another minute, they were scrambling up the bank on the north side of the river.

On dry ground, the horses stood spraddle-legged, blowing hard. The bay shook himself and splattered water on Tim, but Tim was already thoroughly wet and didn't care. He was worried about the pack horse, which was coughing with its head down. Quickly, with water squishing in his boots, Tim untied the latigos on the pack saddle, unbuckled the breeching and the breast collar and pulled the load off the horse's back. Gradually, the coughing subsided.

"Jaysus H. Christmas," Tim said, using a phrase he had often heard from White Shirt Higgins. "We look like a bunch of drowned rats." He glanced at the sky and was grateful for the bright sun. "Won't take long to dry off, though, and we'll go find that herd and then the town and some good feed."

He lifted his sixgun from its holster, flipped the cylinder out, and looked down the barrel. "Wet," he muttered. "Worthless." Unloading the gun, he placed the cartridges on a nearby rock to dry, then looked at his rifle. It was wet, too. He started to unload it, then changed his mind. "Wouldn't do to have both guns unloaded at the same time."

Boots squishing, he walked to the top of the nearest

rise and looked north. Nothing man-made was in sight. It's a damned cinch those fellers know where they're going, he mused. They're not driving a bunch of cattle cross-country without a destination in mind. Has to be a town. Has to be the town of Rosebud.

He went back to his horses, saw they were feeling good enough to crop the grass, and reloaded the pack horse. The pistol cartridges were still damp as he shoved them into the gun. Mounted again, he rode to the top of the hill, paused, looked, and went on, following the wide trail left by a hundred head of cattle.

An hour later his feet were still wet, and he considered stopping, building a fire and drying his boots and socks. That was, if his matches would burn. Hadn't thought about that. Had to get to town or stop somewhere before the sun went down and let the matches dry out. He was in the timber again, going over a low hill. As usual, before he got to the crest of the hill he dismounted and went ahead on foot, keeping low.

The cattle were down there, about two miles away, milling. The rustlers were holding them in a bunch for some reason or other. He counted the riders. Three.

Uh-oh, Tim said under his breath. "There's supposed to be five men and a boy. Something's funny." Slowly, he backed away from the top of the hill and turned back toward his horses. The bay was looking to the west, its head up and its ears twitching. As he grabbed the Winchester from the saddle boot, Tim could feel the hair rising on the back of his neck, and he looked in the direction the horse was looking.

Oh, God, he muttered. He hit the ground rolling the same instant the first shot was fired. More shots

48

followed, and bullets thudded into the ground as Tim rolled up to his pack horse. He stayed down, looked under the horse's belly, and saw one of the thieves behind a tree, jacking the lever down on his rifle. No use shooting back now. He had to find some cover. Desperately, he looked for cover, and behind him saw a shallow ravine full of chokeberry bushes.

Still clutching his rifle, he rolled over and over until he fell into the ravine. Bullets followed him and one kicked dirt in his face. On his hands and knees now, he crawled through the bushes, looking for a hiding place. Stopped. Can't hide. Got to shoot back.

He took his hat off, hoping that would make him more difficult to see, and looked over the top of the ravine. A man carrying a rifle was running toward his horses. Tim aimed his rifle, squeezed the trigger.

Click.

The hammer hit the cartridge, but nothing happened. Still wet. Damn. Tim jacked another cartridge into the firing chamber, aimed, and squeezed the trigger again. This one fired, but he had aimed too fast and missed his target. The shot had one good effect. The thief stopped running and dropped onto his belly.

Levering in another shell, Tim aimed at the tree where he had seen a gunman, squeezed the trigger. Another harmless click.

Scrambling footsteps told him someone was running to his right, trying to get behind him. He dropped the rifle and grabbed the sixgun out of the holster on his hip. A pair of denim-clad legs went past the end of the ravine and a bullet slammed into the ground behind him. Tim fired at the legs.

He heard a noise behind him, and he spun in time to

see a man aiming a rifle at him. He snapped a shot at the man and threw himself to one side as another lead slug clipped branches off the bushes near his head.

Quiet returned. Tim crawled backwards, wanting to get as far under the brush as he could, trying to hide again. Dammit, he reminded himself, can't hide. They know I'm in here. He waited, sixgun cocked, looking for something to shoot at.

The silence held.

What would White Shirt do, Tim wondered. Stand up and fan the hammer of his sixgun? Go down fighting? That's what he'd do, all right, but that would be dumb. Shooting wildly wouldn't accomplish anything. No, best thing to do is stay right where I am. Stay still. Moving, I'm easy to spot. Let them make the next move. Stay right here and hope I can get one of those sonsofbitches before they get me.

Still quiet. He was surprised at how his mind was working. His hands were steady. He was calm. They had him trapped in the ravine, but they had to hunt for him. Come on, he said silently. I just dare one of you sonsofbitches to show yourself. Move where I can see you and you're dead.

Now he was thinking like a gunfighter. A killer. Hell, he was no killer. Too much like his mother. So they said. He had never known his mother. She had died two hours after he was pulled, squalling, into the world. He had lived on wild cow's milk until he was big enough to chew. A succession of grannies. They came and went, just like the rest of the hired help on the HL. No one could get along with White Shirt. The last one had left when he was four, and from then on he was treated like one of the hired help himself. Except when he went to school.

John and Mable Jennings had treated him all right when he'd stayed with them in Shiprock. They had known his mother and sometimes talked about her. What they couldn't understand was why she had married a cattleman and left her comfortable home in Denver. She just wasn't cut out for the frontier life, and White Shirt soon realized he'd made a mistake when he'd married her. Mrs. Jennings had once confided that John "White Shirt" Higgins and Elizabeth Higgins had often gone for days without speaking to each other. She had wanted to move to the city, and he had refused. They probably would have separated if she hadn't discovered she was pregnant.

The poor woman was miserable, Mrs. Jennings said, and dying could have been a relief.

White Shirt had buried her on a hill overlooking the ranch buildings, and he never talked about her, except when he accused his son of taking after her.

If she were in the predicament he was in now, what would she do? Give up and die? According to her husband she had been no fighter. And neither was their son.

Oh, yeah. Maybe she'd never had to fight. Maybe if she was in his predicament she'd fight like a wildcat. They say the most dangerous man in the world is a coward when he's cornered. You never really know how a man will fight until you try him. That applies to women, too. Now the son of Elizabeth and White Shirt Higgins was cornered, and he, by God, was going to fight.

Come on, Tim said under his breath. Show yourselves, you thieving sonsofbitches.

The silence remained. The sun was getting low in the west. They'd have to do something soon. They couldn't be dumb enough to let it get dark before they got rid of the man who'd been following them. In the dark he could get away. Any minute now, they would start shooting.

And then it began.

Hell opened up. Rifles were cracking and at least one sixgun was booming. Bullets thudded into the ground and screamed off the rocks. They knew he was in the brush but they didn't know exactly where. They didn't need to know. All they had to do was fire enough shots into the brush and they'd hit him. They were firing as fast as they could lever cartridges and pull triggers.

Tim moved only his head, and through the branches of the chokeberry bushes he saw a man standing on the edge of the ravine pointing a rifle in his direction. He aimed down the short barrel of his Colt .44 and fired.

Now they had him spotted, and the bullets came closer. Knowing he had no chance at all, Tim fired until the hammer of his Colt fell on an empty chamber.

Then it was over.

Chapter Seven

Dark. He heard himself groan. Pain shot through his temples when he tried to move. His head was a steady, throbbing hunk of pain. He tried to move again. Couldn't.

A match flared and was held close to his face. Couldn't see beyond the match. It sputtered and went out. A dim form was bending over him. He tried to say something, but only groaned again.

It took a lot of will power to move at all, and then he could only turn his head. A small fire was burning on the ground about ten feet away.

Or was it burning in his head. Felt like it. Another groan came out of him. Something wet touched his face. Wet and cool. A hand turned his head and something wet and soft touched his left temple. Wet and soft and soothing.

"Uh. Oh." That was all he could say.

He tried again to move, to raise up. A hand pushed against the center of his chest, pushed him down. A voice said, "Don't." That was all.

"Wha . . . what?" He couldn't just lie there. Had to get up. He tried again. A dizziness settled over him. His ears rang like a church bell and his head pounded even louder. He felt himself fall back. Hard. And then the pain began to subside. His eyelids were suddenly very heavy. Couldn't keep them open. The throbbing in his head slowed.

That soft wetness covered his eyes. The voice said, "Sleep."

A strange voice. Soft. Kind of . . . what? He tried to think. Thinking was too hard. Too hard . . . too hard . . . too hard. . . .

The tops of the trees were the first thing he saw. At first they were fuzzy, but gradually, as he blinked, they came into focus. The sky was blue. A dull pain beat at his left temple.

He sat up, wondering why he was lying on the ground covered by a duck jacket. Where was he? Shakily, he got to his feet and saw the fire. Two fires. One on each side of him. He couldn't remember building them. He must have, and they had kept him from freezing during the night. But still he was cold. Shivering, he took a step, then another. Kind of weak. God, what a head. What had happened?

A boy came out of the woods carrying an armload of broken tree branches. The boy stopped, looked him over carefully, then approached.

"How do you feel?"

A young boy, about fifteen, with an immature voice.

"Feel? I, uh, don't know. What happened to me?"

"You were shot." The boy dropped the wood beside

54

the nearest fire.

Tim's fingers went to the left side of his head, felt the raw, sore spot. "Shot? How?"

"You don't remember?"

"No. Uh, who shot me?"

"You've got a concussion. We've got to get you to a doctor. I'll get my horse." The boy disappeared into the woods. A slight figure, baggy denim pants held up by a tight belt. Big, high-crowned, floppy-brimmed hat pulled down to his ears. Boots and spurs.

Tim took two steps, grunted, and fell to his knees. His head was swimming. The boy came back, leading a saddled horse.

"Can you stand up, Mr. Higgins?"

"Huh? Oh, yeah, I can stand." He got up and stood drunkenly.

"I've only got one horse. You ride and I'll lead him. I think it's about eight miles to town."

"One horse?" He tried to remember. "I've got some horses."

"They took them."

"Who?"

The boy didn't answer. Instead, he led a brown horse up to Tim and held it by the reins close to the bit. "He's fairly gentle, but I don't think he'll carry double. See if you can get on." When Tim hesitated, the boy urged, "Get on, Mr. Higgins. You need a doctor."

Feeling weak, Tim took the saddle horn in both hands and put his foot in the stirrup. With a grunt, and with the boy's hands pushing on the seat of his pants, he got astride the saddle.

"Hang on. We're going."

Tim hung on while the boy went to the fire and

stomped it out. He hung on when the boy picked up the reins and started walking, leading the horse. The boy looked back. "Are you okay, Mr. Higgins?"

"Yeah, Uh, how come you know my name?" His head had quit throbbing and was now a steady hunk of pain.

"I've known you a long time, Mr. Higgins."

"Uh, who are you?"

The boy didn't answer at first, only kept walking, leading the horse. Tim had to hang on to the saddle horn with both hands.

"Do I know you?"

"Yeah, you know me. You used to."

"What . . . what's your name?"

The boy looked back while he walked. "I'm Ellen Olsen. My mother worked in the mercantile in Shiprock. We went to the same school, only you were two grades ahead of me."

"Ellen Olsen?"

"You'd remember if your head wasn't hurt."

"Ellen Olsen is a girl."

"Yeah."

"Well . . ." A wave of sickness swept over him and he almost fell off the horse.

Ellen Olsen stopped. "Can you hang on?"

"I . . . sure, you bet."

"I'm not so sure." Her eyes studied him, and she reached a decision. "All right, I'm going to get up behind you. This horse might throw us both off, but I've got to get you to a doctor as quick as I can. It's a gamble we have to take."

"Why, uh, what's wrong with me?"

"Like I said, Mr. Higgins, you were shot. The bullet

56

cut a groove over your left temple. You've got a concussion and you might be bleeding into your brain. Don't you remember your lessons from school?"

"Naw, I . . ."

"Take your left foot out of the stirrup, will you?"

He did. She put her foot in the stirrup, and holding the reins in her left hand and grabbing the cantle with her right, she crawled up behind the saddle. The horse humped its back and kicked up its heels, but she held on and held him on. "Whoa, Brownie," she scolded, "behave your damned fool self."

She urged the animal forward. It was looking at the humans on its back and it moved with quick, jerky steps. "Behave, dammit." Gradually, the hump came out of its back and its steps leveled off into a smooth, rapid walk.

"Whew," the girl said. "For a minute there I thought we both were gonna be put afoot."

Tim was hanging on to the saddle, trying to think. Ellen Olsen. Oh. Sure. Her mother was a widow who worked in the mercantile. A clerk. Lived in a two-room shack on the edge of Shiprock. Sent the little girl to school in homemade dresses, a coat made out of a blanket, and stockings that were always hanging slack. The kid never could keep her stockings up. Tim tried to look back. Was this really Ellen Olsen? He got only a glimpse of the short nose, the straight, firm mouth and chin. Could be. But Ellen Olsen was a towhead. If this is Ellen Olsen . . . she's got her hat pulled down so low nobody can see her hair.

"Uh, are you . . . ?" It was coming back to him now. The cattle thieves, the gunshots. "How did you, uh . . . ?"

"I'm one of the rustlers. Didn't you guess?"

"You are?"

"Just hang on, Mr. Higgins."

Another wave of blackness covered him, and he felt her arm tighten around his chest.

For an hour they rode, Tim trying to hang onto consciousness, the girl holding him in the saddle. Once, when his head partially cleared for a minute, he said, "If you're a rustler, why are you doing this?"

"It's better than digging a grave."

Other times when he asked something, she remained quiet.

She's a girl, all right, he thought. The arm around his chest had a soft, feminine feel. The hand that clutched the front of his shirt to keep him from falling had busted fingernails, but it was small and feminine. And her breath on the back of his neck had that good woman smell. Yep, she was a girl.

But most of the time he was only vaguely aware of where he was and what was happening. When they rode into a town, he knew there were people around, talking, asking questions. He knew when she reined up and said, "Is there a doctor here? This man is hurt." He felt the horse moving, stopping again. The hands helping him down, men's hands.

"I can . . . walk," he mumbled.

He was lying on something soft, a bed. A ceiling overhead. In a room. He turned his head. She was standing beside him. There was a man in the room, but he left. She bent low over him.

"Listen, Mr. Higgins, I want you to know something. Can you hear me?"

"Uh, yeah."

58

"It was Joseph Holt who saved you. Remember that. He was the one who put his ear to your chest and told the others there was no heartbeat and you were dead. He was the one who came back and took me with him and carried you out of the gulch. He had to get back to the others, but he let me stay with you. Remember that, will you. No matter what happens, remember it was Joseph Holt who saved you."

She stopped talking, and he mumbled, "Yeah. Joseph Holt. I know a man named Joe Holt."

The ceiling dissolved before his eyes, and when he blinked his vision clear again, she was gone.

In her place was a man. Young, bareheaded, a moustache. He looked down at him. "Is your name Timothy Higgins?"

"Yeah."

"I'm Dr. Marvin. That boy, or girl, or whoever, left in a hurry. Can you tell me what happened?"

"I was shot."

The doctor inhaled audibly. "Shot? It looks like you were hit on the side of the head with an axe. When did this happen?"

He was vaguely aware of the girl returning, standing there a moment, then saying, "Give this to him, will you please?" She was gone again.

"When did this happen?" the doctor repeated.

Trying to think, he answered haltingly, "Yesterday . . . or last night . . . I believe."

"Uh-huh." The doctor was turning Tim's head, examining the wound. "You're very fortunate, you know. If this happened last night, then we can be reasonably certain you're not bleeding inside your head. That would have been fatal before now. How-

59

ever, we'll have to keep you here for a time."

The doctor left for a few seconds, then was back. "Hold still now." He felt something soft and wet on the side of his head and heard the doctor murmur, "We'll shave the hair away, then we'll stitch you up."

Later, he heard, "This will hurt. Try not to move."

He tried. He gritted his teeth. His hands balled into fists and his toes curled. Every muscle in his body was tight. A long groan came out of him, but he was determined to lie still.

Finally, "There. Sixteen sutures. You're a brave man, Mr. Higgins. How old are you?"

"Twenty-one. Almost."

"Rest now."

The bed was soft. Nothing had ever felt better. First time on a bed in . . . how long? Lost track of time. Sleep. Wait. Not yet. Joseph Holt? I know him. Knew him. Rode for the HL until he froze his left hand. Had to be amputated. What happened after that? Can't remember. Can't think. Can't . . .

Chapter Eight

It was still daylight. Or was it daylight again? Seemed like he'd slept a long time. Timothy Higgins moved his eyes first, then his head. Still hurt, but not as bad. He tried his hands. They worked. Then his feet. That was when the door opened and the doctor came in.

"Well, I see you're awake now. How do you feel?"

Tim tried to raise up. "I, uh . . ."

"No, don't get up. Not yet. In a few minutes, when my helper gets here, you can go to the toilet if you feel like it. But not without help."

The pillow was soft and clean and smelled good. He really didn't want to move, anyway. But he had things to do. "Uh, doctor, is there a sheriff here?"

"No, but there is a deputy. He's not in town now, however. Had a train robbery yesterday and he's out there somewhere."

"A, uh, train robbery?"

"Yes. The Colorado Central comes through here every Tuesday morning on its way to Jackson, the

61

county seat."

Tim raised up on one elbow. "And it was robbed?"

"Yes. The engineer and fireman were tied up and four passengers had their money taken, but nobody was hurt."

"Is there a stockyards here?"

"On the west side of town. The train was held up east of town about five miles. Nobody knew about it until noon. Someone saw the engine and a string of cars just sitting there and saw the passengers walking along the tracks."

"Do you know, doctor, if any cattle are in the pens?"

The doctor thought it over. "No-o-o. I don't think so. I usually hear about it when somebody is shipping livestock."

"Oh." Tim fell back onto the pillow.

"Here comes my helper. He'll walk you to the toilet, then you can wash up and eat something."

The doctor's helper was a short, husky man with a round, smooth-shaven face and a curl-brimmed hat. Jackboots and overalls. He took hold of Tim's shoulders and helped him sit up. Dizziness came over Tim, but it passed in a few seconds. With the short man pulling on him, he got to his feet, then sat down again.

"I can't go anywhere barefooted."

"Oh, excuse me, of course not," the doctor said. "Jake, help him get his boots on."

The boots were pulled on, spurs and all, and Tim stood again.

"Okay," said Jake. "We'll walk slow and easy."

At the toilet, fifty feet from the back door of the house, Jake stood outside while Tim went inside. Later, when they were walking back, with Jake's shoulder under Tim's left armpit, Jake said, "I hear you was shot. Doc said if the bullet came a hair closer you'd be dead. Said it left your skull in one piece, howsomeever."

"Yeah."

"Know who shot you?"

"Not exactly. Three were shooting at me. Maybe more."

Jake shook his head. "You're one lucky feller."

Looking up at the sky, Tim noticed that the sun was in the west, and he asked, "What time is it?"

" 'Bout three o'clock, I reckon."

"Did I sleep that long?"

"You shore did. But the doc said that was a good thing."

The meal Jake brought him was mush of some kind with a thick slice of bread and apple butter. Tim cleaned up every ounce of it. He felt stronger, but, he grinned to himself, he wasn't up to running foot races. Before he lay back on the bed, he said to Jake, "I've got to see the sheriff or the deputy."

"Yeah," Jake said. "He wants to talk to you, too. But I don't know when he'll get back."

By evening, after he'd slept a few more hours, Tim sat up unassisted. His head throbbed, but his vision was clear and his mind was working. The room was turning dark as he swung his feet off the bed, wondering if he could make it to the toilet by himself.

"Huh," he snorted aloud. "By myself? What kind of baby am I? Can I go to the toilet by myself? Huh." He stood, then sat down and pulled on his boots.

The short walk seemed like a mile, but he made it there and back, and soon after that the doctor came in, lit a lamp, held it close, and studied the wound. "Did a good job, if I do say so myself. I call it my baseball stitches." He chuckled, "I'll bet your head feels like a baseball that was knocked clear out of the field."

Tim managed to chuckle with him. "I never thought of myself as a home run, but that's the way I feel, all right."

"You'll feel better in a few days."

"A few days? That long?"

"Can't make it heal faster."

"I can't stay here a few days. I've got to get going. Is the deputy back yet?"

"I don't know. I think he'll come over here when he gets back. Meanwhile, I think you're able to eat some good beef soup now. Good food will do you more good than anything else. And plenty of rest."

More rest. The window outside the room turned dark. Jake brought in the soup, steaming hot. So hot Tim had to blow on each spoonful. Then another trip to the toilet.

He lay awake a long time, wishing the deputy would show up. Finally he went to sleep.

The deputy came about midmorning. He was a tall galoot with a scrawny neck and a prominent adam's apple. He looked at Tim with sad eyes over a long nose and a drooping moustache. "They said you was shot. Is that right?"

"Yeah." It took a while, but Tim told him all about it, then asked, "Did you happen to see any tracks left by a hundred head of cattle?"

"Naw. Wasn't lookin for 'em, though. Where do you think they'd be?"

Tim opened his mouth to answer, then realized he

didn't know. He didn't know which direction he'd come from. He worried about that and asked, "Did you see which way we came into town?"

"Naw. Didn't see you myself, but folks said you were on a horse with a boy. The boy hightailed it for some reason or other. I can find out."

"Whichever way it was, the cattle were somewhere behind us. Not far. Couldn't be very far."

"All right, I'll find out and I'll go see if I can cut their sign."

Tim was sitting on the edge of the bed. He stood and reached for his boots. "I'll go with you. If I can borrow a horse. They stole mine."

"I don't think you can. Doc says you're gonna have to stay still another day or two."

"If I can get these boots on, I can ride a horse."

The deputy shook his head. "Naw. Can't go against the doctor's orders."

Tim was about to argue when the door slammed open and a man hurried in, breathless. "Deputy Rauer, the bank was just robbed. Just now."

"Aw, shit." The lanky deputy spun on his boot heels and clomped across the floor to the door. His sixgun and holster were slapping his right hip as he left on the run.

Dropping onto the bed again, Tim said with disgust, "Aw shit is right."

A day later he had another problem: no horse and no money. His pockets were empty. He apologized to the doctor. "I owe you a lot, and I intend to pay you, but I can't pay for anything right now. I don't know what I'm going to do." Then he had an idea. "Is there a telegraph office here?"

"Over at the depot."

"Maybe I can wire Aunt Josephine in Denver. If there's any way she can do it, she'll send me some money. There's no railroad in Shiprock and no telegraph." Silently, he vowed he'd never ask his dad for anything, anyway.

"Do you feel like moving?"

"Yeah. Got to."

It was four blocks to the depot, and he walked slowly, carefully, afraid the darkness would return. He'd lost his hat and was bareheaded, and he carried his chaps and spurs, the only things the thieves had left him besides his clothes. Couldn't put a hat on his sore head, anyway.

The town of Rosebud looked pretty much like the town of Shiprock where he'd gone to school—frame buildings of rough lumber and false fronts, a dirt street, smooth now in dry weather. A brick building a block down the street. And the railroad. The Colorado Central depot was easy to spot. Another wooden frame building, but with a better grade of siding and better-quality shingles on the steep roof.

Inside, he found a wrinkled little man wearing a green eyeshade and garters on his sleeves, sitting at a desk behind a long counter. He explained what he needed, but the little man only shook his head. "No Western Union here. Got one over to Jackson, but not here."

"Is there any way my aunt can wire me some money?"

" 'Fraid not. What I can do is send her a message. She'll get it tonight. And she can send you a check on the next train and you can cash it over to the bank."

"When is the next train from Denver?"

"Next Tuesday. Comes through every Tuesday and goes back on Thursday. A day late this week, though. 'Cause of the robbery. She'll go back today."

"Today? How much is the fare to Denver?"

"Seven bucks. That's ten cents per mile."

"Damn. Dammit anyway."

He was walking toward the bank, hoping that by some miracle he could borrow seven dollars on just his signature when Jake caught up with him.

"Doc said to find you and send you back."

"Yeah, I know. I can't pay his bill. I can't pay anything."

"He's got somethin' for you. Don't know what it is."

"Well." Tim felt weak. "I'll go see what he wants."

He apologized again. "I'm sure sorry, doctor. I'll pay you as soon as I can. If I could get to Denver, I've got a bank account there, and I could send it back to you. Or bring it back."

"You'll find a way," the doctor said. "Meanwhile, I forgot to give you something left here by that boy."

"He—I mean she—left something?"

"Yes. I should have given it to you sooner, but it just slipped my mind. I don't know what you want with it." He left the room and was back in ten seconds. "Here."

What he handed Tim was a bandana, a wild rag, the cowboys called it, something the girl had worn around her throat. Black silk. Tied in a knot.

"Well, for . . ." Shaking his head sadly, he held it in his hand and looked at it. "Why did she think I'd want this? After all they stole from me, she leaves me this."

He stuffed it in his hip pocket. "I apologize again, doctor."

"I understand. What will you do?"

"I don't know. I've got to think of something."

Outside, he headed for the bank again, then, feeling weak, he shrugged his shoulders in a hopeless gesture and turned toward the depot. There was a waiting room there. At least a man could sit down. Should have asked the doctor for a loan, he thought; then, naw, he's done enough for me.

He walked a few more steps and muttered, "Jaysus H. Christmas, what the humped-up hell am I gonna do?"

A cold sweat had broken out on his face by the time he reached the depot. He dropped onto one of the wooden benches, feeling sick.

"Do any good?" the agent asked across the room.

Shaking his head, he answered, "No."

"Train's comin in about an hour. She's on time. You can set your watch by 'er. It's mostly downhill from here to Black Hawk, and only another eleven miles to Denver."

Tim reached for the bandana to wipe his face. He untied the knot in it, shook it out, and gasped. A piece of green paper fluttered to the floor. He picked it up, unbelieving.

It was a ten dollar bill.

Chapter Nine

The train was a short one, pulled by a thirty-ton locomotive with six drive wheels, two pilot wheels, and a balloon stack designed to catch the cinders. There were one pullman passenger car, four flat cars stacked high with lumber from a sawmill somewhere, and that was all. No stock cars and no waycar. Only six other passengers.

They kept their faces glued to the windows and were awestruck at the way they traveled, going downhill. The wheels click-clacked over the bolted fishplates that held the rail sections together.

"Must be goin' thirty mile an hour," said a man in stockman's clothes.

Another passenger wore a business suit and a derby hat, and carried a heavy suitcase, which Tim guessed contained samples of something the man was selling. "They'll slow her down to a crawl when we get to the Georgetown Loop. Wait till you see the Devil's Gate Viaduct. I never saw anything so high."

Tim was feeling too weak to wonder at the marvels of

modern transportation, and he settled back in the pullman chair and closed his eyes. It wasn't the first time he'd traveled by rail. He'd gone clear to Gunnison on a train twice, and had traveled by stagecoach the rest of the way to Shiprock.

This train stopped twice to take on water before it got to Black Hawk. There, it picked up two gondola cars filled with ore from the mines, then started on the last eleven miles to Denver. Passengers who thought the Devil's Gate was scary really sucked in their breaths when the train went down Clear Creek Canyon. It hugged the creek in places, and climbed along the high, narrow roadbed that had been hacked and blasted out of a steep rock wall. The engineer and brakemen were applying the brakes and holding the speed to about five miles an hour. If the brakes failed, the train would be a runaway. As if that wasn't scary enough, the salesman in the derby hat allowed, "What we've got here, folks, is a big rolling steam plant. If things don't go right, the whole shooting match can blow sky high."

Tim had traveled by rail over the Boreas Pass farther south, the highest railroad pass in the nation, and he wasn't so impressed. Besides, his head was aching, and the two sandwiches he had bought from a trainman hadn't settled too gently on his stomach.

It was dark when the train puffed into Denver's Union Station, and Tim, carrying his spurs and chaps, had to work his way through the crowd that was always milling inside. Outside, he found a one-horse carriage and driver and paid seventy-five cents for a ride to his aunt's house on Pearl Street. En route, he looked up at the six-story mercantile buildings on Sixteenth. Though he had spent over two years in Denver, he was still amazed at the buildings, the electric lamps, the green lawns, and the crowds of people. Then he saw something he hadn't seen before: electric street cars.

"When did that happen?" he asked the carriage driver.

" 'Bout four months ago. Danged things make too much racket."

An entirely different world from the town of Shiprock and the HL Ranch.

For a moment he feared his Aunt Josephine wasn't at home, but finally she opened the glass-paned front door. A coal lamp inside illuminated her tall, slender frame, in a high-neck dress with puffy shoulders and a skirt that came to the floor. She had her dark hair pulled back in a bun, as usual.

"Timothy? Is that you?"

"Yes, Aunt Josie, it's me."

"Well, come in this house. What are you doing in the city?"

He stepped inside, into the lamplight, and his aunt gasped. "What in the world happened to you? What's wrong with your head?"

He fingered the bandage and shrugged. "I'll tell you about it, Aunt Josie, but it's a long story."

"Sit down. Are you hungry?"

Grinning weakly, he said, "I could eat, all right."

"Well, you just sit right there and I'll fix you something. Are you all right? You look kind of peak-ud."

"I'll live."

He sank into a soft upholstered chair, and she went into the kitchen. He could hear her place a pot of some kind on the coal-burning cookstove. Leaning his head back against the chair, he looked around the room. The

71

same as it had always been. Wallpaper with a flower design, oak floor with a flower-patterned rug covering most of it, but leaving it bare around the edges. Dark-stained walnut furniture: a dining table, four chairs, a cabinet with etched glass panes filled with china dishes and crystal glasses. A long upholstered sofa and two stuffed chairs. A large walnut oval frame held a picture of her late husband, Tim's Uncle Wilbur.

"Did you bring some luggage, Timothy?" His aunt was back. "What happened? Did you get hurt at the ranch?"

"No, Aunt Josie. I was shot."

She gasped again. "Shot? How on earth . . . ?"

"I was trailing some cattle thieves. A doctor in Rosebud said I'm gonna be all right."

"Well, you don't look so good." She headed for the kitchen again. "I've got some soup on. After you eat I want you to tell me all about it."

He slumped in the chair and closed his eyes. Thank God for Aunt Josie. She was the widow of a railroad engineer who had left her enough savings and insurance to live comfortably, though modestly, in her four-room house on Pearl Street. When Tim had left the HL in anger, she had taken him in and seen that he had food and shelter while he looked for a job in the city. "I know Mr. Higgins has mistreated you," she had said. "The same way he treated Elizabeth. He should have known she wasn't the right kind of woman for him. And," Aunt Josephine shook her head sadly, "Elizabeth should have known better, too. You're welcome to stay here, Timothy. It's the least I can do for my poor dead sister."

Then he'd received the first letter from White Shirt

Higgins, saying he was needed at the ranch, that he was a cowman anyhow, not a goggle-eyed clerk in a store. He'd gone back, and he'd stayed through the terrible blizzards of 1886 and '87, the blizzards with a drought between them. In spite of the hardships, he had to admit to himself that he liked the outdoors, good horses, and cowboys. In the city, he'd always felt enclosed and crowded. He was never comfortable in the city.

But White Shirt hadn't really changed, and Tim left again. He had been happy to get his job back at Daniels & Fisher, and he had resumed the life of a city dweller—until he got the second letter. This time old White Shirt said he was sick and didn't have long to live. Tim had gone back, but when he'd asked about his dad's illness, White Shirt had refused to talk about it. At times, Tim doubted he was sick at all, but he did see pain in his dad's face once or twice. Briefly. The rancher had turned his back and tried to conceal it.

"Would you like to eat in the kitchen, Timothy?" Aunt Josephine was standing in the kitchen doorway.

"Yeah." He stood slowly, feeling old, went into the kitchen, and sat at a small wooden breakfast table. The soup, with vegetables and pieces of chicken, was good, and it made him feel better. He stayed in the kitchen and told his aunt everything that had happened. She was all sympathy, and she frowned when he mentioned White Shirt Higgins.

"It just goes to show you can't tell anything about a person till you've known him a long time. I was with Elizabeth when she first met Mr. Higgins. He was handsome, and uh, yes, he was charming. He was different. Kind of, uh, interesting."

73

"Mrs. Jennings told me once that my dad was a pretty decent sort before he was married. It wasn't until he found out my mother wasn't the kind of woman he wanted that he started getting mean."

"Well, he didn't have to take it out on you."

They were silent. Then she asked, "Who is this Ellen Olsen that you mentioned?"

"She's a girl I used to know in school."

"What makes a child do a thing like that? Become a thief, I mean."

"It was her dad, her stepdad, that is. I knew him pretty well. He was a top hand on the HL until the blizzard of eighty-six." Tim shivered when he remembered. "He . . . we were all out that day, trying to pull cattle out of drifts and keep them away from the river. When we got back to the bunkhouse, Joe's hands were white with cold. And when they started to warm up, his left hand turned black and it hurt so bad he couldn't do anything but hold it between his knees and grit his teeth. There wasn't anything we could do for him for two days, and then we managed to get a light wagon to Shiprock. His hand had to be amputated."

"Oh, how terrible."

"That isn't all. He got well and got a hook for his hand, but John fired him because he couldn't do as much work as a man with two hands. Joe homesteaded a hundred and sixty acres around a spring about ten miles from the HL buildings where some of John's cattle watered, and now he and John hate each other."

"I can understand why he hates Mr. Higgins. Isn't that all government land, and can't he take up a homestead if he wants to?"

"Sure. That's why the stockmen hate the homesteaders. They fence off some of the prime pieces of territory. I know darn well that Joe picked that spot just to get even with John."

"But what about this girl, this Ellen?"

"Oh. Well, Joe married a widow named Olsen, and Ellen is the widow's daughter. I saw her a couple of times when I was working cattle. She's the only help Joe has and she does a man's work so much she looks like a man. A boy, I mean."

Aunt Josephine clucked and shook her head sadly. "The things that go on out there. A body would think there was no God further west than the city limits of Denver."

"There is. He shows it more there than He does here, Aunt Josie. You know He's there when you see a new calf take its first breath, or a colt, or when you see a baby rabbit and the first green grass in the spring. Sometimes you have to hunt for Him, but that's true in the city, too."

"You know, Timothy, that's exactly what your mother once said, right after she married Mr. Higgins. You do have your mother's good qualities. Thank God for that."

"Yeah." He was feeling morose now, and he sat with his elbows on the table and his chin in his hands.

"But that don't explain how that child got to be a thief."

"Oh. Well, Joe's a mavericker. We all know that, but nobody has been able to prove it. And I reckon she just followed him. I never knew him to steal more than one or two head at a time, though."

"A what?"

"Mavericker. Some of the calves are missed in the

75

spring calf roundup and after their mammies wean them it's hard to prove who they belong to. Joe, and a lot of others, too, makes a practice of looking for mavericks, and when he finds one he slaps his own brand on it. John has us all riding all the time, but he claims nearly two hundred thousand acres, most of it in rough country, and we miss one once in a while."

"Does he really own that much land?"

"Naw. He was the first to settle there and he thinks of it as his. But as far as I know he has only about a hundred thousand acres deeded. He's buying more, though, and I don't really know how much he's got."

They were silent, and Tim was thinking about the soft bed in his old room, the room he had abandoned twice. Then Aunt Josephine said, "It's too bad about that child. She has to have some good in her or she wouldn't have done that for you."

"She saved my life. But," he added sadly, "she's a thief."

After a breakfast of sausage and eggs the next morning he felt strong enough to walk downtown, to Sixteenth and Seventeenth Streets and to the First National Bank. Except for the downtown district, the streets hadn't been paved with bricks, but they were dry. Dusty, but dry. At times during the dry spells, when traffic was heavy, the city people complained about the clouds of dust that hung over their homes and they urged the city government to do something about the dirty air. And when the streets weren't dusty, they were muddy.

He'd opened an account at the First National two

years earlier and added to it until he had ninety-seven dollars. Now he drew it all out and closed the account. He was feeling weak and his head was throbbing again, and he looked for a place to sit down. It was ironic, he thought, out in the hills where civilization hadn't changed things, a man could sit down or lie on the ground anyplace. Here in the city, if he sat in the street or on the sidewalk, people would think he was a bum and a cop would chase him away.

He walked as far as Twelfth and Broadway, feeling weaker and sicker by the minute, and when he looked up the hill toward Pearl Street he doubted he could make it. It would be embarrassing to pass out in the street. He should have tried one of those new electric street cars. Well, there was only one way to get back. He started up the hill.

Twice, he had to quit walking and try to stop his head from swimming. Dammit, he said under his breath, I should have known better. The doctor told me to rest longer. Nobody to blame but myself.

His footsteps were nothing more than automatic habitual movements when he reached Pearl Street, and by the time he got to Aunt Josephine's house he was only vaguely aware of where he was. His aunt helped him inside and to the bed. She helped him pull off his boots, clucked sympathetically, and scolded him at the same time. "I'm going to send for a doctor."

"No," he mumbled, "don't do that, Aunt Josie. I'll be all right in a minute. Just need to rest a minute. Just a minute." It was evening when he woke up.

After supper he took a bath in a long tin tub in the water closet, crawled between clean white sheets, and slept until after sunup. At breakfast, he said, "I've got

77

to go back."

"Why, Timothy?"

"I've got to find those cattle and my horses. I've got to go back and buy a horse and see if I can pick up their trail. I thought they were going to load the cattle in stock cars at Rosebud and ship them to the stockyards in Denver, but they didn't."

"Why can't the sheriff, or whatever passes for law enforcement out there, find the cattle? It's his job."

"He's got his hands full. First a train robbery, and two days later a bank robbery. I'll have to do it myself."

"And," she looked at him accusingly, "get yourself shot again."

All he could do was shrug.

Chapter Ten

He felt stronger now, and he walked all the way to Larimer Street and Sixteenth. In a saddle shop there he bought a used saddle, sold by some cowboy who had come to the city, run out of money, and hocked his saddle to get eating—and drinking—funds. "You can buy a horse anyplace," he told the saddlemaker, "but used saddles for sale are harder to find."

"Can't ride very far bareback. Unless you're half Indian."

He bought a new felt hat at the same store and set it on the right side of his head.

A street car stopped for him at Seventeenth and Larimer and he rode the jolting, swaying contraption to East Colfax and Pearl Street. He held the saddle on his lap to make room for another passenger, a man, who got on at Seventeenth and Curtis.

"Denver's growing." Tim commented by way of conversation.

"Got near fifty thousand people now. So they said in the newspapers."

"That's a lot of people to gather in one place."

"She's a-growin'. Expect there'll be sixty thousand or maybe even seventy thousand in another ten years."

He carried the saddle from East Colfax to the back porch of his aunt's house, crossed the stirrups under the skirts, and tied them there to keep them from flopping when he carried it on a train. "I'll wait till tomorrow and try to catch a rattler to Black Hawk or Central City, then go horseback from there. Can't get a ride to Rosebud till next Tuesday."

"I wish you'd stay here, Timothy."

"I appreciate everything you've done for me, Aunt Josie. I might be coming back again. I just don't know whether I can live with my dad."

"You just bring yourself on back here and maybe you can get your job again and you won't have to freeze to death every winter out there in that godless place."

He changed the subject. "Has anybody used that stable out back lately?"

"Well, there was a man lived across the alley that kept a horse there for a while, but not anymore. He doesn't have a stable at his house. Why?"

"Just wondered. The street cars don't go everywhere, and a man can walk himself to death in the city."

He deliberately kept the conversation away from his mission, but in the morning when he started to leave, carrying the saddle, she brought it up again.

"I don't understand why you're doing this, Timothy. You've been shot, and you could be shot again. They're not your cattle, anyhow. Let Mr. Higgins get his cattle back himself."

"I don't know, Aunt Josie. I guess it's because those beeves are my responsibility. If I'd been riding in the right territory they wouldn't have been stolen."

She hugged him and kissed him on the cheek. "Be mighty careful, Timothy. If you were younger I wouldn't let you go, but you're at the age where I can't tell you what to do." A tear rolled down her cheek. "I lost my sister and I lost my husband, and I don't want to lose you, too."

"You've been wonderful, Aunt Josie. You're the only relative I've got who . . ." He didn't finish what he'd started to say, but he knew his aunt had shown him the only tenderness he'd ever known. Instead, he said, "I'll be back. That's a promise."

He picked up his saddle, walked to East Colfax, and hailed a carriage.

Black Hawk was a wide-open mining town, with noisy saloons, ladies of both the genteel and over-painted kind, and streets that were even more crowded than Denver's. Miners in jackboots and gentlemen in spats and brocaded vests with gold watch chains, stepped aside and into the gutters to make room for the women. Tim had no trouble finding a horse trader. The message covered the entire wall of the biggest barn in town:

LIVERY HORSES AND CARRIAGES FOR HIRE
HORSES AND MULES BOUGHT AND SOLD
ROBERT RIPP, PROP.

"I got the horses, if you've got the money," said the owner, a man in a high-crown flat-brim hat, with a waxed handlebar moustache. "Big or little, black or white or in between."

He led Tim to a feedlot behind the barn where a dozen horses stood, looking bored. "Huh," Tim snorted, surprised. "I know that horse. That's my horse."

The animal he pointed at was old Spook, his gray pack horse.

"Cain't be," Robert Ripp said. "I bought 'im from a cowboy that was down on his luck and needed the money."

"When did you buy him?"

"Why, just yestiddy. Paid sixty bucks for 'im."

"How much?"

"Sixty bucks."

"Take a look at his left shoulder. What brand do you see?"

"It looks like an HL."

"Ever hear of that brand?"

"Cain't say I have."

"Well, I'll tell you." Tim crawled between the corral poles and walked up closer to the horse. The livery owner followed. "The HL outfit is in Parker County and the brand is registered with the Secretary of State. You bought a stolen horse."

"Nossir. I got a bill of sale in my office."

"What about the bay?"

"What bay?"

"I had two horses stolen from me. This one and a bay. Both carried the HL brand. Who did you say you bought them from?"

"I didn't buy no bay horse. And I bought 'im from a gentleman name of Benjamin Jones."

"What did he look like?" Tim realized he was firing

questions at a man, something he'd never done before, but then he'd never been shot and had his horses stolen before.

"Now see here, boy. You cain't accuse me of buying stolen horses. Like I said, I got a bill of sale."

"What you've got is a piece of paper signed by a thief. Anyone can sign a bill of sale. Is there a sheriff here?"

"He's out of town. He's electioneering."

"Has he got a deputy?"

"Yeah. You gonna get the law?"

"You bet. That's my horse and I want him back. Would you know where I might find the deputy?"

"Now see here, you'll have a hard time provin' that animal was stole from you. And I got good money tied up in 'im."

Tim crawled out of the corral. "I'll get the deputy."

"Wait a minute. Wait a goddamn minute, will you?"

Tim looked blankly at the man.

"Like I said, I got good money tied up in that horse, and you'll have to go to court to prove he's yours." The man pulled gently at one end of his moustache, then reached into his shirt pocket for a sack of tobacco. "I think we can save us both some money and a whole lot of time." He began rolling a smoke.

"How?"

"Let me ask you, where you headed?"

"West. To Rosebud."

"In a hurry to get there?"

Tim had a hunch he shouldn't answer that question, and he hesitated.

"Reason I asked," said the horse trader, exhaling a lungful of smoke, "the judge here is awful busy. Might take till next week before he'll listen to you. Then the sheriff'll have to wire the state gov'ment, and then you'll have to wait your turn in court again." He paused and took another drag from his cigarette.

His message was clear. If Tim wanted to go to court and prove the horse belonged to him, he was going to have to stick around Black Hawk a week or more to do it. And the livery owner had him pegged. He couldn't wait.

But he wasn't giving up. Not yet. "I'll go get the deputy."

"Maybe we can work out a deal."

"Huh? What kind of deal?"

"I'll let you have 'im cheap. That way I'll get some of my money back and you can be on your way."

"How cheap?"

"Like I said, I paid sixty bucks for 'im. I'll let you have 'im for forty."

"Forty?" Tim had a hunch the man had paid less than forty. Horse traders had an unwritten license to lie. They knew every trading trick there was and they didn't consider it a disgrace to use every one of them.

"I'm losin' twenty dollars."

"Can't do it," Tim said. "I'd be losing forty. That's my horse, and I'll be damned if I'll pay to get him back."

Another drag on the cigarette, then, "Oh, you'll pay, all right. One way or the other. Listen, you're purty young to be dealin' with the law, and you can bet your bottom dollar I ain't givin' up a horse I paid good money for without the judge tells me I have to. I got a lawyer workin' for me, and he knows how to sweet talk the judge. If you're smart, young feller, you'll pay forty dollars and be glad to do it."

84

He was right, and Tim knew it. It would cost him at least forty dollars in the long run, and he'd waste a lot of time, besides.

"Tell you what I'll do," he said, trying to talk like the horse traders he'd seen in action, "I'll give you ten dollars. That's ten dollars more than you'll get if I go to court. And if you hire a lawyer, you'll have to pay him, and you'll lose. I can prove that horse belongs the HL outfit, owned by John Higgins, and I can prove I'm John Higgins's son."

The cigarette was dropped onto the ground, and a boot heel stomped it out. The livery owner squinted at Tim. "You're a smart kid, ain't you? Nobody likes a smart kid."

Turning as if to go, Tim said, "I'll go find the deputy."

"Fifteen dollars."

Tim stopped, looked back. "Nope. Ten"

"Fifteen or we go to law."

Now it was Tim's turn to squint. "Are you sure you didn't buy a bay horse, too?"

"Nope. That feller left here a-walkin'."

"How about a saddle? Did he sell you a saddle?"

"Nope. Said he sold the saddle to somebody else."

"Did he say who? Or where?"

"Nope. Didn't ask."

"What did he look like?"

"Are you gonna give me fifteen bucks for that horse?"

It was the best deal he was going to get, Tim knew. The horse trader had probably paid no more than forty dollars for old Spook, and he had to get some of his money back to save face. Not that the horse wasn't worth more. The trader had no doubt read the seller's mind and had known he wanted to get what he could right quick and be on his way.

"All right. Fifteen dollars. And you won't have to make out a bill of sale. I can prove he belongs to me." He reached for the roll of money he carried in a shirt pocket.

"Feller I bought 'im from was short, kind of heavy set. He had a round face. Looked like he had some Injun blood in 'im. If you catch up with 'im give 'im a kick in the ass for me."

"I'll do that. Now tell me something else. You seem to be a man who knows what's going on around here. Have there been any cattle shipped from here in the last few days?"

"Nope. None that I heard about, and you're right, I know just about ever'thing that happens in these parts."

"Have you heard of a herd of cattle, about a hundred head, anywhere around here?"

"Nope. And if they was around here, I'd hear. Not many cattle shipped from here. Too many men're gittin' rich diggin' holes in the ground."

Tim saddled and mounted the gray horse named Spook and rode away from the livery barn, trying to decide what to do. The short, heavy man who had signed the name Benjamin Jones wouldn't stay around Black Hawk. Too easy to find here. Probably headed for the big city where a man could hide. And spend money. If he'd sold a stolen horse here, the cattle had to be around here, too. Where? On some ranch? In somebody's feedlot, eating corn and getting fatter?

And what had become of Tim's good bay saddle horse? The thieves had probably ridden him to Denver. Trying to find him in Denver would be almost impossible. Forget the horse. For now, at least. Find those cattle. How? A hundred head of cattle can't disappear. If they weren't shipped by rail then they're somewhere west of Denver. The only way to find them was to pick up their trail again. Starting at Rosebud.

"Well, Spook, old feller, we've got a ways to go."

Chapter Eleven

He stopped at a dry goods store and bought two wool blankets, then at a grocery store where he bought a long loaf of rye bread and seven cans of preserved foods, including some tinned beef, and a box of matches. When he rode past a gunsmith's shop, he stopped and looked in the window at a Winchester repeating rifle, much like the one he'd lost, and he mentally counted his money. Nope. Hate to be unarmed, he mused, but not much money left. Might need it worse than I need a gun.

At another store he bought a long skinning knife and a belt holster for it, and at a saddle shop he bought a pair of leather saddle bags and a thirty-foot grass rope. Then he was on his way.

It took two days to get to Rosebud, and every time he saw humans he stopped and asked if they'd seen a herd of cattle. No, they all said.

He'd eaten five cans of preserved food and the saddle bags were lighter by the time he got there. The sun was low in the west. He stopped first at the doctor's house and paid him. The doctor was surprised to see him.

"I'm always patching up transients," he said, "and it seems that very few can pay for my services. Apparently, they think I'm supposed to work for nothing, because they almost never come back. But the townspeople have said many times that they need a doctor here, and they see that I have everything I need."

His next stop was at the deputy's office and the town jail, but the door was locked. He had started to untie his horse from a hitchrail and leave when he saw the lanky deputy walking toward him.

"Hey there, young feller," the deputy said, "thought you'd left the country."

"I still want to find those cattle," Tim said. "Can I talk to you a minute?"

"Shore. Come on in." The deputy unlocked the door and led the way inside. He plopped down in a swivel chair behind a big desk and propped his feet up on an open desk drawer. A one-cell jail with steel bars was behind him, and a slouchy skinny man with a three-day growth of whiskers got up from a steel bunk, came to the jail doors, and hung on to the bars with both hands.

"Don't say anything," the deputy warned his prisoner. "No bellyachin'. The judge said thirty days, but he'll be gone day after tomorrow, and I'll let you out then. If you keep your mouth shut."

To Tim, he said, "That judge comes around here once a week or so from Denver, and he treats drunks like they was some kind of desperados. He's a teetotaler himself, and he thinks ever'body else ought to be like him. I always did believe the damned judges ought to get locked up in jail theirselves once. Maybe then they wouldn't be so damned quick at ordering people thrown in jail. Besides, it cost money to feed jail prisoners."

"It's no disgrace to get drunk," Tim allowed. "It might be against the law, but it's no disgrace. Not for a working man, anyhow."

"You a drinkin' man, son?"

"Oh, I've had a few drinks of whiskey, but I don't make a practice of drinking."

"That's the smart way to feel about it. Now," the deputy settled deeper in his chair, "what can I do for you today?"

Tim dropped into a chair beside the desk. "I don't suppose you found any cattle carrying the HL brand."

"No, son, I haven't. I been tryin' to run down a couple gents that robbed the bank, and I plumb lost their trail, and I been tryin' to figure out why some other gun-slingin' sons-of-bucks held up the train."

"Which way did the bank robbers go?"

"They left town goin' west, but they doubled back up there in the hills and went east. Hell, they're in Denver now, living high on the loot."

"Did you get any kind of description of them? Or their horses?"

"Not much. They had them wild rags over their faces, and their horses was both bays. Like most horses. They looked like cowboys, the way I heard it. You know, chaps and spurs and big hats. But that fits the description of a hundred other men around here."

"Well, you've had your problems. I don't suppose you had any help?"

"Shore. The sheriff was here for a couple of days, and I had some good men from town here."

"But no sign of any cattle?"

"No. I got to admit, I been so busy with ever'thing else that's happened I haven't been looking for your cattle."

"But you've been looking for the bank robbers' sign on both side of town?"

"Yep."

"And you didn't see any sign of cattle?"

"Nope, but that don't mean anything. There's a lot of country where a bunch of cattle could be hidden."

"Did you ask anybody which way I—we—came from? I was so damned sick at the time I didn't even know where I was."

"Yeah, I did find that out. You came from the east. You and that boy. Who was that boy, anyway?"

Tim lied, "I don't know. I don't remember much of what happened, only that I was trailing some cattle thieves and somebody shot me."

"You goin' after 'em again?"

"Yeah. Got to."

"That's dangerous. Want some help?"

"No-o-o." Tim thought it over. "Not right now. When I find them I'll need some help. But not right now. Which way is the river?"

"About eight miles south."

"What is it, the Colorado?"

"Naw. It's the Blue River. We're a long ways from the Colorado."

Standing, Tim said, "I'm not as far north as I thought."

Outside again, he mounted the gray and rode slowly out of town, heading east, back the way he had come. "Wish I could put you up in a barn tonight, old feller, but I can't afford it." He stopped suddenly and went

91

back to town, to a general store. There, he bought seven more cans of preserved food, stuffed them in his saddle bags, and rode out of town again. "No telling when we'll see civilization," he said to the gray, "but we've got to find those cattle."

He didn't go far before darkness forced him to camp for the night. He found a grassy spot and staked out his horse, ate a can of dried beef, and wrapped up in his blankets. For a long time he lay awake, wishing he had a couple more blankets and his bed tarp and wondering what was ahead. He remembered swimming a river, then climbing a hill on foot and seeing the stolen cattle about two miles away. He hadn't known at the time where he was or which way the town of Rosebud lay. But the deputy had said he and the girl had come into town from the east.

"All right," he said to himself, "all I have to do is find that river, then I can find the spot where I crossed it, and then I can find the spot where I was shot." He realized he was talking to himself and wondered whether being alone so much was driving him crazy. Then, "Naw. Lots of men live alone in cow camps where they don't see anything human for months, and they don't go crazy." He chuckled when he remembered one cowboy's comments on the subject. "It's all right to talk to yourself," the cowboy had said, "and it ain't too bad to answer yourself. But if you get so mad at the answers that you haul off and punch yourself, you'd better go to town."

*   *   *

A stiff, cold wind came up during the night, and Tim shivered when he unwrapped his blankets. He pulled on his boots, stomped his feet and waved his arms to get warm. Up on the side of a hill to the south of him the aspen leaves were turning yellow, and the clumps of aspen among the pine and spruce made yellow spots on the hillside. He built a fire to get warm, but ate a cold breakfast. He had been told that canned food had to be consumed very soon after the can was opened or the food would make a man sick. "Should have bought a skillet," he said to himself. "Getting damned tired of cold chuck."

The horse was cropping the high country grass, oblivious of the chilly air.

His meal over, Tim saddled up and mounted. "The river is about eight miles south, that deputy said. I don't know the country around here and I don't see any trails to follow, so we're going to have to climb some mountains, I reckon. Let's go."

Horse and man climbed the hill by traversing it, stopping four times to blow. Finally at the top, Tim dismounted and loosened the cinches to let the horse breathe a little easier. All he could see from there were more rocky, timbered hills. Glancing at the morning sun to be sure he was going in the right direction, he tightened the cinches, mounted, and rode down the hill, across a narrow valley and up another hill.

When the sun reached its highest point, he stopped, loosened the cinches again, and let the horse graze while he ate another can of dried beef. "Can't be much farther to the river," he said. "Not if it was only eight miles. It's eight hard miles, but we ought to get there pretty soon."

Two hours later they came to a hill they couldn't climb. It was solid rock and almost straight up. The rock looked like it had been put there in layers. Tim studied the country in all directions, and finally turned east. "That girl brought me from somewhere around here," he said to the horse. "Somewhere around here there's an easier way."

It took another hour to find a dim trail going south, and he sighed out loud. Ought to be better traveling from here on, he mused. The trail led him around the rock cliff, between two steep hills, across a creek, and over a low, aspen-covered ridge. From there he saw the river.

"The Blue River, that deputy called it," Tim said to himself as his horse walked and slid down a steep hill toward the water. "Never heard of it. But there's a lot of rivers I never heard of."

When he reached the water he knew where he was. "I crossed down there, about a mile from here. I remember looking up here and seeing the river coming out of that canyon over there." He reined his horse east and followed the river until he came to where he'd swum across.

"Recognize this place, old feller? Don't worry, you won't have to swim today. I don't think so, anyway."

From there it was easy to find the spot where he'd been shot. Empty shell casings were scattered all around the brushy ravine where he'd holed up. He knew it was a miracle that he had been hit only once, considering all the shots that had been fired, and he wondered if he'd hit anybody. Apparently not. He had been the doctor's only patient. Unless he'd killed somebody, in which case the thieves had probably just buried the body or dumped it in the river and gone on their way.

He went to the top of the hill he'd climbed after he'd crossed the river and picked out the area where he'd last seen the stolen cattle. Then, back at the scene of the gunfight, he found the remains of the two small fires the girl had built to keep him warm during the night he should have died.

It was late afternoon when he got to the cattle trail. He could see that it had rained sometime since he'd seen the cattle last, and he reckoned it had hailed, too. Hail preceded rain very often in the high country. The trail could still be seen, but the weather had eliminated most of it. "All right," he said to himself, "hoofprints aren't just jumping right up at me, but a hundred—make that four hundred—hooves are bound to leave marks on the ground that a little rain and hail can't wipe out."

The trail went east, away from the town, parallel with the river, but about a mile north of it. Traveling was easier. The thieves seemed to know where they were going, but their destination was a complete puzzle to Tim. He followed the trail until close to dark, then camped for the night near a small stream. Not worried about an ambush now, he built a fire, opened a can of beans with the skinning knife he'd bought, and put it in the fire, top side up. Food heated in the can had to be eaten immediately, he'd been warned, and soon he wrapped the bandana the girl had left him around his hand, picked the can out of the fire and shoveled the beans into his mouth. The loaf of bread he'd bought had only a few small green spots on it, and he ate a hunk of that, too.

95

The horse, tied by one forefoot with a thirty-foot rope, was making a meal out of the mountain grass. "Someday we're going to quit living like this," Tim said to the animal.

He found a spot under some lodgepole pines where the pine needles were thick on the ground, picked out the rocks, and curled up in his blankets, taking off only his boots. For a long time he lay awake, looking at the stars between the treetops and listening to the night wind sigh through the trees. Though he missed his bedroll with the thin mattress and the long tarp doubled back over him, he was fairly comfortable, and he admitted to himself that he enjoyed sleeping out. He enjoyed the sound of the wind and he enjoyed hearing his horse blow its nose and crop the grass.

"But," he grinned in the darkness, "I've got to quit talking to myself. I've got to find somebody more interesting to talk to."

The next day he found someone. Someone who was certainly interesting. Someone like no one he'd ever met before.

Chapter Twelve

The cattle trail went over a low rise, between two hills, and through a stand of pines and spruce, and Tim found himself back at the river again. Instead of crossing the river, the cattle had followed the north bank until the river went into another narrow, rocky canyon. From there they had turned north and gone through dense woods. Once out of the woods into a grassy park, Tim could see where the thieves had let the cattle graze for a day.

He stopped there and ate another can of beans. He was ready to mount up and go on when he saw someone coming toward him. Someone walking.

For a moment he stared. The someone was a quarter mile away, too far to be recognized. He, she, or it, seemed to be staggering. It fell to its knees, got up, and staggered on.

"Uh-oh. Looks like somebody's hurt," Tim said to the horse. "Let's go have a looksee."

The figure staggered on, stopped suddenly when it saw Tim. It waved its arms and yelled something unintelligible. Tim booted the gray into a lope.

"Jaysus H. Christmas," he said when he got closer. "It's a girl."

No mistake about that. She had long dark hair, and wore wool knickers, black wool stockings, a checkered shirt, and a wide belt that showed how small her waist was. She was bareheaded.

Tim dismounted on the run and grabbed the girl just as she was about to collapse. "Wh . . . what?" That was all he could say.

Her lips parted and she mumbled, "Thank God."

Gently, he lowered her onto her back and looked down at her. "What happened? You lost? Get thrown from your horse?"

"Lost," she gasped. "Three days. No horse."

"How . . . ?" Then he realized the girl needed help, not a lot of questions. What to do? Finally, he asked, "Are you hurt?"

"No. Not hurt. Just so . . . so very tired. And hungry. Starved."

"Hungry? Well, I can do something about that. Just stay here and I'll build a fire and heat up something to eat."

He went to his saddle bags and picked out a can of beef hash. They were in the open, away from the trees, but the trees weren't far away. "Wait here. I'll get some wood. Just stay right here. I'll be back in a couple of minutes."

She sat up when he mounted the gray, and her face was filled with horror. "Please. You're not leaving? Please."

98

"No ma'am, I'm not leaving. Just going to get some wood to build a fire."

"Please."

"Don't worry. Tell you what I'll do. I'll leave my horse here. Would that make you feel better?"

She didn't answer, just stared at him.

"I'll be right back." Tim dropped the reins, knowing old Spook would crop the grass but wouldn't go far. He left on a dog trot toward the woods. Fortunately, the lodgepole pines always had dead limbs at the bottom, which made good firewood, and soon he gathered an armload. Back with the girl, he dropped his load, used his skinning knife to cut a piece into splinters, and within a few minutes he had a fire going.

The girl only watched, hugged her knees, and said nothing.

"It isn't much," Tim said, "but it'll keep a feller alive." When the can was warm, he lifted it out of the fire and handed it to her. He went to his horse, took a tin spoon out of the saddle bags, and handed that to her. "Eat it quick. It won't keep more than a few minutes in the can."

"I know," she said. "What is it?"

He thought that was a strange question for a starving person to ask. But he answered, "Says on the can it's beef hash. It's got some pieces of potatoes and stuff in it."

"Oh."

He watched her eat. After the first few tentative careful bites, she ate faster until she emptied the can.

"Feel better?"

"Much. Do you know where we are?"

"We're south and east of the town of Rosebud."

"How far?" She was pretty, with a perfectly formed mouth and soft brown eyes. About his age.

"Two days."

"Oh." Her shoulders drooped even farther and her eyes took on a glazed look.

"You say you've been lost three days?"

"Yes."

"And you've been walking all that time?"

"Yes."

"Well, no wonder you're dog tired. I've been hungry, but I've never had to walk that much. How'd you get lost?"

"Hunting. With my father."

"Hunting? Elk?"

"Yes. My father loves to hunt and he always wants me to go with him."

"And you got separated somehow?"

"Yes. I couldn't find him."

He digested that and asked, "Where do you live?"

"In Denver."

"Have you been in the mountains much?"

"A little. As I said, my father loves to hunt and sometimes I go with him."

He could see the fatigue in her face as she crossed her arms over her knees and rested her chin on her arms. Without looking at him, she asked, "Can you help me?"

"Well, sure. Uh, can you ride a horse?"

"I've ridden some."

"That horse over there is plumb gentle. You ride and I'll walk. I think if we head straight north we'll come to the road that leads to Rosebud. Maybe a wagon'll come along."

"Do you think it will take two days?"

"Not to the road. Probably a day and a half. We'll both be hungry, but we'll make it."

A long sigh came out of her and she looked at him with worried eyes. "I . . . I'll have to rest. I'm very tired."

"Yeah, sure. Maybe we ought to stay here tonight and start out in the morning. I've got a couple of blankets you can have. I'll sleep by the fire."

"I hope I'm not . . . keeping you from anything."

He decided to lie. "Naw. I'm just looking for some cattle. I can pick up the trail later."

"I'll pay you for your trouble. My father will."

"Naw."

It was the time of year when the flies weren't so bad, and she was able to rest comfortably on his blankets on the grass. He busied himself gathering more firewood, and when he carried his second armload to where she was resting, he saw that she was asleep. He carried more wood until he believed he had enough to last the night. Then he was restless.

He wanted to stay on the trail of the stolen cattle, fearing he had already lost too much time, but he couldn't leave her, either. He studied her as she slept. A pretty girl. The longer he looked at her the more he was convinced of that. She was lying on her right side with her knees drawn up and her long dark hair covering most of her face. No way to mistake her for a boy. The wide belt pulled her clothes in at the waist, and her knickers and checkered shirt flared out from the belt in the nicest feminine curves he had seen in a long time. A very pretty girl.

But, dammit, what was he going to do with her? He frowned at the ground, looked over at his horse, and frowned at the ground some more. Well, there were two alternatives. He could point her in the right direction, give her his food and blankets and send her walking, or he could go with her. If he gave her his food and blankets he would starve or freeze himself. Besides, she might get lost again. She was a city girl, and maybe didn't know north from up or down. And she was scared. When she had thought he might leave her she was terrified. He could have been the ugliest, meanest sonofabitch in the world and still she would have been glad to see him.

And besides all that, he had been alone too much lately, and she was really something to look at.

Damn, he said to himself, isn't she something.

She woke up at sundown and jerked to a sitting position. Her eyes were wide and her mouth opened, but the only sound she made was a sudden intake of breath. He was sitting cross-legged ten feet away. Her eyes took in the country around her, the trees, rocks, grass, the horse. Him. She had that terrified look on her face again.

He smiled, trying to let her know he was nothing to fear. It was a forced smile, but it helped. Slowly, recognition came to her eyes, and she stammered, "You, uh, you're the nice young man who, uh, gave me something to eat."

"Yes, miss." He stood. "I think we'd better stay here tonight. I haven't got much chuck, but I'll share what I've got, and we won't starve before we get to the road.

Unless you feel like heading out now. We've got another hour before dark."

"Oh, uh." She got to her feet. "I feel stronger now. Now that I've had something to eat and some rest. Thank you very much."

An hourglass figure. That's what it was called. Then he was ashamed of himself for thinking thoughts like that. "Well, we can't go very far in an hour, and we might not find another good spot like this to spend the night. There's water over there." He nodded to his left. "There's good grass for the horse and everything we need."

"Whatever you say. I am tired."

"All right. We'll stay right here and start out first thing in the morning. Are you hungry now?"

She smiled a weak smile. "I don't think I'll ever get enough to eat again, but I can see that you don't have much food. Do you think we should ration it?"

"We'll have to eat light. I was traveling light."

"And you have only two blankets."

"Yeah. You can have them. I'll keep a fire going."

Another long sigh came out of her. "I apologize. I'm really sorry to be so much trouble. It was stupid of me to get lost. Really stupid."

"A lot of people get lost in the mountains. Uh, I was thinking, maybe your dad has some men out looking for you. Maybe we'll meet with them tomorrow."

"Yes. That is a possibility. But that is something I have been hoping for for the last three days, and it hasn't happened."

He frowned at the ground again. "Well, if it happens, fine, and if it doesn't we'll survive anyhow."

"You seem to be sure of yourself. You're obviously

103

an experienced outdoorsman. That's very reassuring to me. How very fortunate I am to have met you."

"Uh, I was wondering, you said you were hunting. Did you have a gun?"

"Yes. A Krag bolt action something or other. It was supposed to be a good hunting rifle. I . . . I'm sorry to say, I lost it. Well, to be honest, I just got tired of carrying it and put it on top of a boulder where I hoped I might find it again."

Tim chuckled. "Someday, somebody'll find it."

"Whoever finds it is welcome to it. I never cared much for hunting, anyway."

He went to his horse, untied it from the stake rope, and led it to the water. When he returned, he noticed that the horse's pastern on the left foreleg was becoming a little rope burned, and he took off his bandana, wrapped it around the pastern, and tied the stake rope to the bandana.

"Got to keep you healthy, old feller. Boy, do we need you."

The girl was sitting beside the fire, hugging her knees. He carried the saddle bags to her and said, "The dinner menu is, well, kind of short. And the chef isn't the kind you'd want to compliment. But pick something, will you, and we'll pretend it's a porterhouse steak."

She smiled. A pretty smile, with white, even teeth. "After the diet I've been on the past few days, anything will be delicious."

She stood and walked into the woods. He guessed the reason and pretended to be busy doing something with his saddle. From there she went to the creek and washed her face and hands.

"We'll have to speak to the management about accommodations," he joked.

They emptied two tins of food, she eating with the one spoon he had and he eating with a wooden spoon he'd carved out of a stick. By then it was dark, and he put more wood on the fire.

Except for the firelight, the world around them was dark, and that gave him a feeling of intimacy. He glanced at her. She was hugging her knees again, staring into the fire.

Just to have something to say, he asked, "Where in Denver do you live?"

"On Washington Street. Not far from the state capitol."

"Washington Street. I know where that is. My aunt lives on Pearl Street, in the same part of town." There were some mansions on Washington, he remembered. But there were some modest homes, too.

"Oh, really? Are you familiar with Denver?"

He told her about living in Denver and working at Daniels & Fisher.

"But," she was puzzled, "why are you looking for cattle?"

Somehow, he didn't want to tell her the whole story, so he answered, "My dad owns the HL outfit. That's in Parker County. Some of his cattle wandered this far. I'm trying to find them."

"Your family owns a ranch?"

"Yeah."

"I don't understand. Why were you working at a dry goods store?"

He shrugged. "Just to see what the city is like."

"And," she added, "I know it's none of my business,

but what happened to your head?"

Unconsciously, his hand went to the bandage. The spot was still sore to the touch. "Oh, it's, uh, I just got skinned up, that's all." He hoped she wouldn't ask any more questions on that subject.

She looked at him curiously for a moment, then looked into the fire. He got up, broke a dead tree limb over his knee, and watched the flames wrap themselves around it.

"By the way," she said suddenly, "my name is Mary Jane McCeogh. My father is Alfred McCeogh."

"I'm Timothy Higgins."

"I'm happy to meet you, Mr. Higgins." She smiled and her face was beautiful in the firelight. Heart-shaped, with a straight nose and a pert little chin. "As a matter of fact, I'm very happy to meet you."

Grinning with her, he said, "To tell the truth, I was getting kind of lonely." His smile widened. "I even got to talking to myself."

He reminded her that she could have the blankets and he would stay by the fire and keep it going, but she disagreed.

"Oh no. You have two blankets. I'll use one and you use the other."

"One blanket won't keep you comfortable."

"It's better than what I've had the last three nights." She shivered. "I didn't realize how cold it gets up here."

"Even in the warmest part of the summer, it's cold at night. And we're heading into winter now."

She stood, picked up one of the blankets wrapped it around her shoulders, and sat again. "Thank God you have matches. A person doesn't realize how important the little things are."

106

"You can use the saddle for a pillow. It's better than the bare ground."

"Oh, really? I've read about cowboys using their saddles for pillows."

"We don't usually. It bends the skirts out of shape. But that's an old saddle. It doesn't matter. I'll use the saddle blanket." He got up and carried the saddle to her, turned it upside down, and said, "There's some of the sheepskin lining left. That'll help."

"Well then, Timothy, I will—how shall I say it—retire for the night." She rewrapped the blanket around her and lay down with her head inside the saddle skirts. "Goodnight, Timothy."

"Goodnight, uh, Mary Jane."

Chapter Thirteen

It was a long, cold night. Twice he woke up shivering, and when he looked at her she was lying on her side with her knees drawn up and her hands between them. Both times he piled more wood on the fire and waited until it put out more warmth before he closed his eyes. Shortly before daylight he looked at her again. She was shivering. He took his blanket and covered her with it. Then he put more wood on the fire and sat up the rest of the night.

The slowly changing colors were fascinating. The first change appeared on the eastern horizon—a faint glow that gradually grew brighter. Then the light spread slowly over the rest of the world. Mountain peaks became visible, and then the woods. He could see sunlight on the peaks to the west. The sunlight moved slowly down the peaks until finally it was shining in Timothy Higgins's eyes.

He got up stiffly, stretched, and sighed. The girl was sleeping, warmed by the sun. He went to his horse, looked at the rope-burned pastern, saw it was nothing serious, and led the horse to the water. When he returned he put the last of his wood on the fire and wished the girl would wake up. It was already late in the morning, and they had a long way to go.

She awakened, and again her eyes were wild. But when they settled on him, she smiled. "Good morning, Timothy."

"Morning."

Stretching, she turned her face to the sun. "O-o-oh, the sun feels wonderful."

"Got kind of cold last night. I hope you got some rest."

"Yes. I can go on, now. Excuse me, won't you."

"Sure."

She took another trip into the woods and then to the creek. By the time she got back he had two cans of peaches opened. "Not my favorite cuisine," he said with a grin, "but it's nourishment."

"Nourishment is the important thing. Right now I could eat a horse raw." She smiled and nodded at old Spook. "You over there, I didn't mean that."

Breakfast over, he stomped out the fire and saddled the horse. "All right, you ride and I'll walk."

"Can't he carry both of us?"

"Naw. Maybe for a short distance, but not all day. That's asking too much of him."

"Oh. We do have a day and a half of travel ahead of us, don't we."

"Yeah." He helped her get mounted, careful to keep his hands off her bottom. He picked up the bridle reins, glanced at the sun to get his bearings, and started walking. After a few steps he stopped, took off his spurs and chaps, and hung them over the saddle horn.

Walking was not his favorite pastime, but there was nothing else he could do. He walked.

She was quiet most of the time, and he didn't feel much like talking, either. Walking uphill was the worst, and he took the easiest route, careful not to lose his directions. Every time he topped a hill he looked at the sun, then picked out another hill or tree or boulder due north and headed for it. His high-heeled boots were made for riding, not walking, and by noon his feet were sore. Well, that's tough, he said under his breath, just keep walking.

They rested at noon and shared a can of beans while the horse cropped the grass. After an hour he said it was time to get going again, and she obediently got on the horse.

Once, she said, "Why don't you let me walk a while, Timothy? You have to be tired."

"Naw." He just couldn't ride while she walked.

"I'm wearing good hiking boots. My father made sure of that."

Silently he wished he could trade boots with her, but he said nothing.

At the top of a steep hill he had to stop and catch his breath. She dismounted. "Please. Let me walk a while."

"Naw. I'm all right."

"Are you sure?"

"Yeah." He was breathing so hard he couldn't have said much more.

"I'm an experienced hiker, really I am."

His breathing returning to normal, he grinned at her. "The first time I saw you you couldn't hardly put one foot in front of the other."

"That was yesterday. I'm rested now."

"I'm rested now, too. If you'll get back on the horse, we'll go on."

She obeyed.

An hour before dark he stopped. "There's some things about the mountains I like and some things I don't like. Climbing these hills is one of the things I don't like, but one of the things I do like is the water. I've heard of people dying of thirst when they got lost on the plains. In the mountains there's always a creek somewhere around."

He was standing near a small stream that had been stronger earlier in the year, but was drying up now. Still, there was water. They were at the bottom of a hill near a stand of aspen. "This is a good place to camp."

She slid off the horse and stretched. "O-o-oh. How can anything full of hay be so hard."

"It isn't the horse that's hard, it's the saddle. But if you think you're sore now, try riding very far without it."

She smiled that pretty smile. "I don't intend to try that, thank you."

He didn't know why she was so cheerful. Maybe it was just her nature to be cheerful. Some people were like that. It made him feel ashamed of himself for feeling grumpy. Trying to pick himself up, he said, "What would madam like for supper? I mean dinner. We have, uh, beef hash cold, beef hash warm, or uh, beef hash with beans."

"Oh, uh." She pretended to ponder the question. "Uh, sir, do you happen to have any beef hash?"

He laughed for the first time—how long? Too long.

"Beef hash coming up."

First he took care of the horse, then he broke off some tree limbs and stomped on some downed aspens to break them into fire-sized pieces and built a fire. By then the sun had gone down and the air was turning cold. He opened two cans of hash with his knife and commented, "One can left. Peaches. Hope we find that road tomorrow."

Their meal over, she stretched out and leaned back on her elbows. He couldn't help staring at her hourglass figure. He forced himself to look away.

"I really like the mountains," she said. "Being lost was horrible. I was terrified. But I really like the mountains and camping out. I inherited that from my father."

He kept quiet and let her talk. The dry aspen trunks popped and shot sparks as they burned. "Hunting is not my kind of fun, though. I don't like to kill anything. Especially the deer and elk. They're such beautiful animals. Do you hunt, Timothy?"

"Oh, I've shot my share of game, I guess. But only because I wanted the meat. Not for sport."

"Yes. Unfortunately, we humans are carnivorous." She was silent a moment, then, "Were you raised on a ranch, Timothy?"

"Yeah. Born and raised on the HL."

"And you went to the city just out of curiosity?"

"Yeah. Sort of."

"Do you like the city?"

"Not very much. It was good to work indoors in the winter where the temperature is always about right, but I missed the outdoors."

"If you had to take your choice, one or the other,

which would you choose?"

"Oh, I don't know. Never thought about it much."

"Is your family's ranch a big one?"

"One of the biggest in Colorado."

"Do you mind my asking personal questions?"

"Naw."

"That's good, because you're one of the most interesting people I've ever met. I'm just dying of curiosity."

He didn't say so, but he was curious about her, too. But asking personal questions was considered bad manners in his part of the country.

"Aren't you curious about me?"

"Well, yes, now that you mention it. What does your dad do for a living?"

"He works for the United States Government, the Bureau of Indian Affairs. He's an Indian agent."

"I've heard of such people."

"He buys cattle and seed grain and things like that for both Ute reservations. The one in Utah and the one in southwest Colorado."

"Uh-huh."

"Now that the Indians are confined to reservations and the buffalo are gone, the United States Government feels it should help feed them."

"I don't always agree with the government, but I can't argue with that. I had nothing to do with killing off the buffalo, but I feel guilty about it just the same."

"Yes. That's what my father says. Wait till you meet my father. You'll like him."

Tim chuckled. "I hope to meet him sometime tomorrow. Before we run out of groceries.

They were silent and she wrapped a blanket around

113

her shoulders. He broke up another tree limb and tossed it on the fire.

"Timothy?"

"Huh?"

"Do you think we'll find that road tomorrow?"

"I'd bet on it."

"Will you be coming to the city in the near future?"

"I might. Yeah, I might end up there, all right."

"Will you come and visit me?"

"Sure."

She lay back and put her head on the sheepskin lining of the saddle skirts. "Goodnight, Timothy."

"Night."

"I'm very glad I met you."

Another cold night, getting up a half-dozen times to keep the fire going. She slept fitfully, too, and he could hear her sighing and turning from one side to the other, trying to find a comfortable position. He put his blanket over her and threw more wood on the fire. Dawn was a relief.

At dawn he got up, stomped his feet, and waved his arms to get the blood circulating. He checked on his horse, went to the trickle of a stream and splashed water on his face. The water was so cold it felt like it was biting his fingers.

By sunup they had eaten the last tin of food, saddled up, and were on their way. His feet were blistered from walking, but he gritted his teeth and walked on. Neither had much to say.

At midmorning, she insisted on getting down and

walking with him. He tried to talk her out of it, but she was determined to have her way. Still, he would not get on the horse. He would not ride while she walked.

They climbed two long hills, one so steep they had to traverse it, and when they got to the top, panting and puffing, they could see a wagon road below them.

"There it is," he said.

"Where? Oh, I see it. Is that the road to the town of Rosebud?"

"Has to be. Let's get down there and hope a wagon comes along."

They walked, slid, and walked. Tim led the horse, and at one point it slipped onto its haunches, but got up immediately. Finally, they were down on the sagebrush flats and on the narrow road that wound between the boulders and the ravines. Grass grew in the center of the road.

"What should we do now, Timothy?"

"Wait right here. Somebody'll come along in a wagon. No use walking any farther."

"Do you really think someone will come along?"

"Yeah. Now that the railroad has reached this part of the country, there won't be a stage or any freight wagons, but somebody has to be going to town sooner or later."

Their stomachs were grumbling as they sat on the ground between the wagon tracks and waited. The horse found some grass among the brush and grazed until it stepped on the bridle reins. It stopped and stood there.

"At least I'm not cold," she said. "But, boy, could I use something to eat."

"Yeah." He grinned. "My stomach thinks my throat's been cut."

"How far do you think it is to town?"

"I'd guess about ten miles."

They were silent as their eyes and ears strained to catch the sound or sight of human traffic. Then she said, "What you ought to do, Timothy, is get on that horse and go to Rosebud and send someone back for me. You ought to do that right now. Someone could get back here before dark."

"I thought of that, but I don't want to leave you here alone."

"Why? I can't get lost again."

"You take the horse. You can handle him. I'll wait."

"No. I'll wait with you."

"This is really a fool thing to do, you know. If you took the horse we'd both be eating a good meal in town tonight."

"Someone will come along."

"Yeah. Surely, sooner or later."

Two hours went by, and the sun started its way down to the western horizon. Tim was getting worried. "I guessed wrong. We should have kept going. The closer to town we get the more likely we'll see somebody."

"Do you think we should resume walking?"

"Yeah." He stood. "I'm beginning to feel like a fool just sitting here."

"But your feet are so sore you can barely stand it."

"How did you know?"

"I can tell."

"Well, I'd rather walk on sore feet than spend another night in the cold without supper."

"I'll make a deal with you. You ride the horse and

116

I'll walk. Otherwise I'm staying here."

She was right, and he knew it. She was more able to walk now than he was. But he also knew that if he was seen riding while the girl walked, he'd be sorely embarrassed.

He was trying to figure out what to do when he saw the wagon.

Chapter Fourteen

She jumped up and looked where he pointed. "But it's coming from the town instead of going to it."

"Yeah. Well, maybe we can bum something to eat."

They watched the wagon approach. It was a light wagon with leaf springs under the seat. Two horses pulled it, and when it came close the horses didn't like the looks of the two-legged animals standing in the road.

Tim said hello to the man and woman on the seat and pulled the girl by the arm off the road.

"Whoa," the man said. He wore a wide-brimmed hat and his boot on the brake handle was a riding boot. A cattleman. "Howdy."

"Howdy," Tim said. "How far to Rosebud?"

The woman, in a shapeless flower print dress, stared at Tim and the girl. Mostly at the girl.

"I'd cal'culate eight mile. Give or take a mile. You lose a horse?"

"No, we only had one to . . ."

The man interrupted, "Say," he was squinting at the

118

girl, "is your name McCeogh?"

"Yes," she answered. "I'm . . . I've been lost up there." She pointed back the way they'd come.

"There's a lot of men lookin' for you. Is your dad Alfred McCeogh?"

"Yes, sir."

"He's been purt' near crazy. Him and a bunch left town yesterday lookin' for you and they ain't been back yet."

"I . . . I'm safe now. Thanks to Mr. Higgins here. But we are tired and hungry."

The woman spoke then. "I'll just bet you are hungry. I can fix that. Bert, open up them groceries."

The man handed the lines to the woman and climbed to the rear of the wagon. He wore California wool pants, the kind that White Shirt Higgins always wore. "We got all kinds of airtights that don't have to be cooked, and we got dried fruit that tastes better stewed but can be ate without stewin'."

He tore open a cardboard box. "We got tomatoes, peaches, beans, and all kinds of stuff. We even bought a dozen tins of oysters. They ain't bad and they'll stick to your ribs."

The woman climbed down from the wagon but held on to the lines. "Hand me that can opener, Bert." He did, and she opened a can of oysters. "Best way to eat these little dickenses is to just let 'em sorta slide down your throat." She handed the can to the girl.

She took the can, reached in with her fingers, took out one of the slippery oysters and popped it into her mouth. Everyone watched as she chewed twice and swallowed.

"Tastes awful at first," the woman said, "but after

119

the first few they begin to taste tolerable."

The man handed another can to Tim, and he soon agreed with the woman. By the time he reached the bottom of the can the oysters were tasting good and his stomach told him he'd eaten some solid food.

Holding out his hand to shake, the man said, "I'm Bertrum Holloway."

They shook. "Timothy Higgins. I was looking for some cattle that were stolen from my dad, John Higgins, over in Parker County, and I saw her wandering around alone. It took us a day and a half to get this far."

"Bert," the woman said, "that's the young man that was shot. I heard about him."

Mary Jane gasped, and looked wide-eyed at Tim. "Shot? Is that what happened to your head? You didn't tell me that."

Grinning crookedly, Tim said, "Aw, I didn't want to make a fuss over it. I'm as good as new now."

"Yeah, I heard you was lookin' for some stolen cattle and got shot by the thieves. No, I ain't seen hide nor hair of 'em. If I did I'd do some shootin' myself. The damn—excuse me, lady—the darn rustlers're makin' it tough for ever'body."

"We calculate we're losing about twenty-five head a year," the woman said.

"That sure takes all the profit out of the cow business," her husband added. "I hear the HL is a purty big outfit."

"Yeah. Where is your ranch?"

"The house is northeast of here about ten miles."

"Then you haven't been riding up there in the high country?"

"Naw. If your cattle are up there, it could take a lot of ridin' to find 'em."

"Here comes some men that've been ridin' up there." The woman was looking west down the road. A half-dozen riders were coming.

They were coming up the road from the east, and when they saw the wagon they booted their horses into a gallop. The girl watched them come, and suddenly exclaimed, "That's my father."

They came up, their horses blowing from the run. The wagon team tried to turn away from them, but the man named Holloway hauled on the lines and got them turned back.

"Daddy."

Her dad was a big, thick-chested man riding a big sorrel horse that looked to be half percheron. He got off awkwardly and grabbed his daughter in a hug. Tears rolled down her face as she wrapped her arms around his neck. He didn't speak for a long moment, then he stepped back and looked her over.

"Are you hurt, Mary Jane? Are you starving? You must be awfully tired. Your mother is worried sick."

"I'm all right, Daddy. I am very tired and I need a good hot meal, but I'm all right. Thanks to Timothy."

Tim stood there, believing father and daughter should be left alone, but not knowing how to excuse himself.

"Daddy, I want you to meet Timothy Higgins. He saved my life."

"Who?" The big man's head swiveled toward Tim. His eyes took in everything about him from the bandage on his head down to the scuffed riding boots.

"I, uh, just happened to see her wandering around up

there," Tim said, then silently chastened himself for offering an explanation.

"What were you doing up there?" The man's voice was not friendly.

"Daddy," the girl pleaded, "he saved my life. I had walked almost as far as I could walk when I met him."

"Oh, uh . . ." He stuck out his hand. "Excuse me, will you. I've been so worried about my daughter I didn't know what I was doing. I'm Alfred McCeogh."

They shook. Alfred McCeogh was thick in the stomach as well as in the chest. He wore lace-up boots and a campaign hat. His face was round and smooth-shaven. That made Tim very much aware of his beard stubble.

"I'm looking for some stolen cattle," Tim said, his gaze going over the men still on horseback. "They're carrying the HL brand."

The men looked at each other. "Haven't seen 'em," one of the men answered. "Haven't seen any cattle."

"Ain't you the feller that was shot by some cattle thieves?" asked another.

Tim didn't answer. Instead, he asked, "How far did you go up there?" For the moment the girl was forgotten and he was only interested in finding the stolen herd.

"We covered a good fifteen square miles." The horseman turned in his saddle and waved a hand in the direction of the south and east. "Went as fur as the river. Didn't think she'd cross the river."

"How far east did you go?"

Alfred McCeogh interrupted, "We've got to get my daughter to town. Do you feel like riding behind me, Mary Jane?"

"Yes, I . . ." She looked at Tim. "Timothy, are you coming?"

"Well, I don't know. I've got to have some chuck. I'm plumb out. Uh, Mr. Holloway, I know I'm asking a lot, but could you sell me some groceries?"

"Yeah, we can spare some."

"Let's go." Alfred McCeogh swung awkwardly into the saddle, lifted his left foot out of the stirrup, and offered a hand to his daughter. She took his hand, put her foot in the stirrup, and climbed up behind him. The big sorrel horse shuffled its feet, but it was easy to handle.

"Old Redbird there is big enough to carry three of you," a rider said, nodding at the sorrel.

"Oh," Alfred McCeogh said as an afterthought, "Mr. Higgins, I want to pay you for your trouble."

"Naw."

"You should let him pay you for your food, Timothy," the girl put in.

"Naw. Forget it."

"I'll be happy to reimburse you. I should have offered to pay you sooner, but I'm so concerned about my daughter that I forgot my manners. You understand."

"Sure." Tim looked up at the riders. "How far east did you go?"

"Thanks, Mr. Higgins," Alfred McCeogh said. "When you're in Denver, look me up. Maybe I can return the favor."

Mary Jane looked at him pleadingly. "Please come to see us, Timothy."

"Sure. You bet."

The riders left. The wagon team wanted to go with

them, and again the rancher had to haul back on the lines. Tim's gray horse took three steps toward the departing horses, stepped on a rein, and stopped.

Tim watched them go. The woman spoke. "She'll be fine. She's a healthy young girl and her dad seems to care a lot about her. She'll be fine."

"Yeah. Uh, Mr. Holloway, I've lost so much time I might never find my cattle, and I hate to lose more time going to town for some chuck. I'd sure be obliged if you could sell me something."

The rancher handed the lines to his wife and stepped to the back of the wagon again. "Help yourself to these airtights and fill one of your saddle pockets with dried apricots. That'll keep you goin' for a while."

Tim went to his horse, untied the saddle bags, and brought them over to the wagon. He took two cans of oysters, two cans of tomatoes, two cans of peas and corn. He half filled one saddle bag with dried fruit. "How much do I owe you?"

"Nothin'. You catch up with them rustlers and get 'em arrested or shot, and we'll owe you."

"Good luck, young man," the woman said. "May the good Lord ride with you."

Tim tied the saddle bags in place and mounted the gray. "Thank you, ma'am."

The rancher chirruped to his team, and the wagon moved forward with a jerk. Tim followed for two miles, to where the wagon road turned south, then he quit the road and continued east, keeping his eyes on the hills to the south. He rode silently, and realized he was alone again. He suddenly felt terribly lonely.

"Dammit," he said aloud, "a man wasn't meant to live this way. Those beeves are so far gone I'll never find them. What the hell am I doing, anyway?"

Then he answered his own question. "I'm doing what I started out to do way back—how long ago? Too damn long ago. It's not the smart thing to do, but like old White Shirt has said a hundred times, I haven't got a brain cell in my head."

He rode on. "Nope. Not a lick of sense."

Chapter Fifteen

From up on a high ridge, Tim looked north and saw the wagon road and beyond that the railroad. His eyes followed the rails until they disappeared between two hills. For a long while he sat his horse and tried to think, to figure out what the rustlers' plan had been. Or still was.

They'd lied to that farmer about driving the cattle to Rosebud and loading them in railcars, that was for sure. They'd stayed south of Rosebud. They'd lied just in case someone came along asking questions. Like Tim Higgins. So where had they gone? He wondered if he could pick up their trail again. Sure. Why not? He'd had some luck. No rain. Not while he was following tracks, anyway. The tracks have to be still there, he thought. South. But those riders rode all over the country to the south, looking for a lost girl, and they didn't see any cattle. How far east did they go? Didn't say. Come to think of it, he'd asked, but got no answer. That overfed gent interrupted every time he'd asked.

Should he go back to where he'd first seen Mary Jane

McCeogh and pick up the trail there? Or could he save time and miles by heading east as well as south? He mulled it over and concluded: the answer is simple, go east and south as far as the river. They wouldn't want to swim the river twice, so they had to be on this side of it. If he didn't cut their sign by the time he reached the river, he'd double back west until he did.

He rode on, dropped into another valley, crossed it, and climbed a gentle timbered hill, angling east and south. The sun was at his back now as he rode, apologizing to the gray gelding for making him climb so many hills. "But you don't know, old feller, how good it is to be riding instead of walking. I thank you and my feet thank you." When the sun sat on the horizon behind him he looked for water and grass and a place to camp. It was almost dark before he found a natural spring that dribbled out of a stone wall two feet above the ground. With his hands and boot heels he scooped out a hollow in the ground below the spring and watched it fill with water. The horse didn't have to be told what to do. It put its nose in the hollow and drank its fill.

The night air was cold, but two blankets were better than one. Before he dozed off, his thoughts went to the girl. She never complained, did she, he asked himself. In fact, she had treated the whole thing as an adventure. He tried to picture her as she was now, well fed, freshly bathed, and sleeping peacefully in a clean, soft bed. Was she thinking about him? Naw.

He curled up on his side, cradled his head inside the saddle skirts, and slept until daylight.

*　　　*　　　*

127

When he unwrapped himself from his blankets and pulled on his cold boots the next morning, he couldn't help thinking about that warm bed in his Aunt Josephine's house in Denver, and he wondered again what kind of fool he was to be out here looking for cattle that were probably slaughtered by now and their hides burned or buried.

The blisters on his feet complained painfully when he took his first few steps, and he groaned aloud. That reminded him to look at his horse's feet. "Right now your feet are more important than mine," he said to the horse. The steel shoes were showing a lot of wear, but were still thick enough to protect the hooves from the rocks. "Going to have to be reset before long," he commented.

He was grateful for the sun when it showed itself and spread its warmth over the rocky, timbered hills. Heading directly into the sun now, he studied the ground and the country ahead of him. Every time he topped a hill he hoped to see the cattle below him, or at least their tracks. After ten or twelve miles he angled south again, hoping to find the Blue River, if nothing else.

"We might have to go all the way to Black Hawk," he said aloud, "but those cattle couldn't just disappear. There's got to be some sign of them somewhere."

By dark he had found no sign, and he spent another night on the ground wrapped in two blankets. It was noon the next day when he again saw the river. And it was at the river that he again saw the cattle trail.

"Uh-huh," he said to himself. "They came along here and followed the north bank. Wonder how far? And where in holy hell were they going?" He reined up, dismounted, and loosened the cinches.

The canned oysters reminded him of cattle slobbers, but he could feel the slimy mess sitting solidly on his stomach. He tossed the empty can in the river, watched it float away, and wondered idly where it would end up. Then he tightened the cinches, mounted, and rode on.

In another ten miles, the trail turned away from the river and went north over a low hill. From there it went through dense woods and turned east. Tim could tell by the tracks and the color of the droppings that he was about two weeks behind, but getting closer. It was late afternoon when he rode out of the timber, around a pile of boulders, and saw something that caused him to rein up sharply.

The railroad. And something else.

He turned his horse around quickly, went back behind the boulders, dismounted, and went on foot to where he could hide behind a boulder and study the country ahead. Yes, it was the railroad. Part of it, anyhow. It ended right there on the west side of a steep hill. A big hole in the side of the hill gaped at him. It was shored up by timbers and partly hidden in scrub oak. More rails, narrow ones, ran into the hole. A tin shack stood a hundred feet from the hole, back in the lodgepole pines, barely visible from where Tim was. Fractured rock was scattered over the ground between the hole and the shack.

A mine. Gold. Or silver.

Eyes wide, his breath in his throat, Tim studied the scene. Nothing moved. No sign of life of any kind. Not human nor animal. For at least ten minutes, he watched. Then, wishing he had a gun, he made his way forward, carefully trying to make no sound. First he went to the shack. Two rusty ore cars stood on the narrow rails in front of it. The rails were rusty, an indication that they hadn't been used lately. The door of the shack was wide open and the glass window had been broken. Inside, there were two broken wooden chairs and some papers scattered over the floor. Tim picked up a torn and wadded copy of the *Rocky Mountain News*, dropped it, picked up more papers, and saw a piece of a letter that was addressed to the Tall Timber Mining Co.

Outside, he followed the narrow rails to the mine opening. It was black inside. He turned and studied the rails coming from the north. Bright spots on the rails told him they had been used recently.

Still cautious, he followed the rails a hundred yards and found out what had happened to the stolen cattle.

It was all there as plain as day. First he found a loading chute. It was roughly built of pine tree trunks and two-inch lumber, and the wings on each side were built of tree trunks. It had been torn apart and dragged back into the timber, but it was not well hidden. And there were the marks on the ground. The marks told what had happened. The cattle had been there, but not for long. Maybe a couple of hours. Then they had been loaded on to railcars. Tim studied the ground further and followed the rails. Yep, he said under his breath. The railcars had had to be pulled by a two-horse team about three hundred yards, and from there they had rolled downhill. He could see where team had been unhitched and led away by someone on horseback.

There were no other horse tracks. The other horses must have been loaded on railcars, too.

He walked back to his horse, his mind throwing out questions. Where did the railroad cars come from? Where did they go from here? Who had led the team away, and where had they been taken?

He decided to camp out of sight of the abandoned mine and start out in the morning, following the railroad. He used his bandana again to tie around the horse's pastern the bandana that Ellen Olsen had left for him. It didn't sore the horse the way a grass rope would. That left the horse comfortable, more comfortable and better fed than he was. His dinner tasted god awful. Nothing duller than canned peas. They weren't even salted. The oysters were bad enough, but canned peas tasted like cold mush. It took a lot of water to wash down the taste. Oh well, he reminded himself, it was solid food. Barely edible, but food.

During the night a wet fog rolled down from the high peaks, and the grass was wet with dew. Walking in the tall grass was almost as bad as wading in a creek, and his feet were soon soaked. He downed another can of something without paying any attention to what it was. When he put the wet saddle blanket and saddle on the horse, old Spook humped his back and acted like he wanted to buck.

"I don't blame you, old feller, but you've been a mighty good horse. Don't go silly on me now."

The horse took a few rough, stiff-legged steps when Tim mounted, but kept its head up. Soon its back was warmed enough that it went along in a smooth, rapid walk.

Back at the railroad, Tim reined north and followed the rails through a quarter mile of scrub oak, between two hills, and out onto the sagebrush flats. After another mile he saw where the rails joined the main line. A padlocked switch with a long handle could direct railcars off the main line onto the spur that led to the abandoned mine. It could also turn cars from the spur back onto the main line. The padlock was broken.

It wasn't hard to figure out. Some cattle cars, Tim didn't know how many, had rolled downhill from the west, from the direction of Rosebud, had been turned onto the spur line, and had rolled on to the mine. The spur had no doubt been built to serve the mine. Gold or silver ore had once been loaded onto gondola cars there and hauled to a mill at Central City or Black Hawk.

And that was where the HL cattle had been hauled. Not to a mill, but to a stockyard there.

When he thought about it, it all added up. A train robbery east of Rosebud. The passengers were robbed, but that wasn't what the robbers wanted most. That was just extra profit. Some railcars and the waycar had been uncoupled. Gravity had pulled them down here. Someone among the thieves knew how to work the brakes on a railcar and how to throw a railroad switch. If gravity didn't pull the cars all the way to the abandoned mine, a team of horses could pull them the rest of the way.

But, Tim thought, sitting his horse deep in thought, would the loaded cattle cars roll all the way to the railroad stock pens somewhere? And were the brakes strong enough to stop them exactly where the thieves wanted them stopped?

Well, there was only one way to find out. He turned his horse east and followed the rails. Fog limited his vision to fifty yards. The cattle had probably been slaughtered by now, but he had to find out who had stolen them and gotten the money for them.

Or take it out of somebody's hide.

Chapter Sixteen

In spite of the fog, the railroad was easy to follow most of the way, but after an hour he came to a deep canyon. The rails crossed the canyon on a trestle that was supported by long steel legs. A man could walk across that, but not a horse.

Tim looked for and finally found a trail that led to the bottom of the canyon. He reined his horse downhill. The trail was an old one, but it had seen a lot of use when the railroad was being built, and it was easy to travel. At the bottom, Tim looked up at the trestle and whistled through his teeth. "It took a lot of smart to figure out a way to get a railroad up there. It took a lot of educated brains. You have to admire the men who figured that out."

The fog began to clear as he rode out of the canyon. For a while the sun tried to come out, but gave up and hid in the clouds again. He stopped there and let his horse graze while he ate a double handful of dried apricots. Holding up one of the shriveled pieces of fruit, he allowed, "If I don't start eating better I'm going to look like this."

At midafternoon he came to another trestle, but this one crossed a narrow ravine and was short. He followed the tracks where they curved north, went between some hills, curved back south, and continued east. A few more miles of easy traveling, and he came to a steep hill that rose out of a creek. The railroad bed had been blasted out of the side of the hill. Tim rode across the creek and looked for a way to travel parallel with it. Couldn't.

All he could do was try to find a place to climb the hill. He turned back up the creek, crossed over, and looked up. Boulders as big as a barn stuck out of the side of the hill, with bare, gravelly dirt between them. A few sticks of scrub oak grew out of the hill. A man on foot couldn't climb that, much less a man on a horse.

Going back the way he had come, Tim cursed to himself. "Damn. Goddamn. No wonder those stump-headed thieves stole some stock cars. Riding the rails is a hell of a lot easier than climbing these goddamn mountains. Well, old feller, I hate to say it, but we've got to climb. That is, if we see a place where we can climb."

He had to backtrack a half mile before he got around the hill, then he turned east and south. In another quarter mile, the country rose sharply, and again Tim apologized to the horse. "When we get to the top, we'll look for a place to camp," he promised.

It took an hour, but finally they topped out. From there, Tim looked down at the creek and at the railroad hugging it. He vaguely remembered that canyon when he'd traveled by rail to Denver. And that wasn't the worst canyon the railroad went through.

"I changed my mind, old feller. We need some water. I do, anyhow. Takes a lot of water to wash that dried fruit down. At least it's downhill from here."

It was nearly dark when they reached the railroad again. They crossed the creek, and Tim staked his horse there and built a fire out of scrub oak. After he'd wrapped himself in his blankets and was settled for the night, his mind went back to the HL and John White Shirt Higgins.

He thinks I'm sitting on my ass in Denver, Tim mused. Or dead. If he thinks I'm dead he's probably sent some men to look for my body. But if he thinks I'm in Denver he's so damned mad he doesn't care what happened.

If I don't find out who stole those cattle, I might as well be dead as far as he's concerned. He'll never believe how hard I tried.

I can't believe it myself.

Well, at least I've learned something about what happened to that herd. I'm learning something every day now. And tomorrow's another day.

The next day was the first day of the winter season in the high country, and Tim had to shake snow off his blankets that morning. It was a light snow, barely covering the ground, but the sky was overcast and threatening to dump more of the white stuff.

"Jaysus H. Something or Other," he muttered, waving his arms to get the blood circulating. "It's still September. I think. It doesn't have to snow this damn early."

But when he thought about it he realized that snow

was better than rain. Not so wet. But damn, it was cold.

"Merry Christmas, old feller," he said as he led his horse to the creek. "Today is the last day of this. Tonight you're going to be chomping on good hay and maybe some grain, and I, by God, am going to be sleeping in a warm bed. Yes sir. Today is the last day of this kind of living."

But by noon he was beginning to have doubts. The fog of the day before had disappeared, and though the clouds were low overhead, visibility was good. He should have seen a town by now.

Instead what he saw was another curve in the railroad. And back among some cedars, almost hidden, was a sidetrack.

The sidetrack was long enough to hold a string of railcars, and when Tim got closer he could see there were two cattle cars and a waycar. He rode up to the waycar, the caboose.

"Hello," he yelled. No answer. "Hello inside the car." Still no answer.

He dismounted and tied his horse to the built-on ladder on the side of a cattle car. Wishing again he had a gun, he approached the rear of the waycar cautiously, afraid to blink, afraid to breathe. He climbed the steps and looked in a window. A wood-burning stove, two bunks, a table, an overhead lamp suspended from the ceiling on a chain. Two chairs. No people.

The door opened on squeaking hinges and he peered inside. No use saying hello.

Stepping down from the rear platform, Tim studied the ground and almost immediately realized what had happened. He pushed his way into the cedars and found the remains of another loading chute. Only this one had been used to unload cattle.

He walked back to the main line and looked west up the tracks. Yep. It had worked as slick as a whistle. The tracks were fairly level for a quarter mile and were on a slight uphill grade from there. The cars had rolled downhill from that spur line, probably pretty fast for a ways, then had slowed when they hit the flats and come to a stop on the sidetrack. Sure, they'd had to twist the brake wheel, but not too much.

In fact, he saw when he went back to the sidetrack, somebody had dragged a heavy tree trunk across the rails to make sure the cars stopped.

He shook his head in wonder. A slick scheme. Worked perfectly. Steal a herd of cattle, drive them over the mountains to a spur line, rob a train, and uncouple some cattle cars, roll them downhill to the spur line, load the cattle, pull the cars with a team of horses to get them rolling again, let the cars roll down here, and unload the cattle.

That much was obvious. The rest was easy to guess.

Drive the herd to the railroad pens at Central City or Black Hawk, load them in railcars again, haul them to the Denver Union Stockyards, and collect the cash.

And no doubt tell everyone they came from a ranch west of Central City.

The sidetrack had to be near one of the two towns. The railroad wouldn't build a long sidetrack very far from town. "Huh," Tim snorted, still shaking his head. "You'd think they built this here just to help cattle thieves. Hidden in the cedars and probably close to town. Damn. Made to order."

"Well," he said, mounting the gray horse, "it's time someone blew up their little scheme. Come on, old

138

feller, let's go to town."

He had guessed right. At the top of the next hill he looked across a pine-studded valley and saw the town of Black Hawk. "Look familiar, old Spook? You've been there before. Come to think of it, that stable hand said he hadn't seen any cattle nor heard of any being shipped. That means they held the herd out of sight of town somewhere and let them graze a few days before driving them to the pens. That jasper who signed his name as Benjamin Jones sold you to get some eating money. Or drinking money. Or both.

"Damn." His jaws tightened when he thought about it. "I was right there in town when those cattle were grazing around here. Damn it all, anyway. If I hadn't been in a hell of a hurry to get back to Rosebud, I'd have been here when they shipped them. I couldn't have missed them by more than a day. I came within a day of catching those sonsofbitches with their pants down."

He shook his head sadly. "The lucky sonsofbitches."

The streets of Black Hawk were still crowded, and honky tonk piano and banjo music came out of one of the saloons. The music could be heard far down the block.

The gray horse had its head up and its ears twitching as Tim rode down what appeared to be the main street. Buggies and wagons almost bumped hubs as they passed, and Tim had to rein his horse between them. A few of the well-dressed men and a couple of the women looked him over as he rode by, but no one said anything to him. He was looking for the sheriff, town marshal, deputy, or any kind of lawman.

After riding down one street, around a corner, and up another street, he turned toward the livery barn. He tied his horse to a hitchrail and went inside the barn. Robert Ripp was currying a paint horse, and he looked up at the sound of footsteps. His eyebrows arched.

"Didn't expect to see you back, young feller. What're you up to now?"

A wry grin turned up the corners of Tim's mouth. "Same thing. Hunting stolen cattle."

"You look like you came through a sick mare backwards. How long since you et?"

Tim didn't answer. Instead he said, "I think my cattle were here. I think they were shipped from here a day or two after I left."

"There was a bunch of cattle loaded at the stockyards, all right. I heard about 'em, but I didn't go over and look at 'em"

"Which way is the sheriff's office?"

"He ain't here. He's electioneerin'."

"Again? What's he getting paid for? Was he here when those cattle were shipped?"

"Don't think so. This is a big country, and we got an election comin' up. If he don't get reelected he'll have to go back to dealin' faro."

"Damn." Tim leaned his buttocks against a wooden box stall and kicked back at the boards with a spur. Old White Shirt was right. When you've got trouble, take care of it yourself. Going to the law was a waste of time. "Well, is there a deputy or a town marshal?"

"Yeah." The stable man went on brushing the paint

140

horse's mane. "Charlie Hoskins is his name. His office is two blocks east and a half a block north. He's appointed and he don't worry about no election."

"What will you charge me to feed my horse tonight?"

"Four bits. If you want oats, that's a dime extra."

"I'll be back."

On the street again, he found a hole-in-the-wall office with a sign on the door that said "Marshal." Leaving his horse tied to a hitchrail, he opened the door and went in. The office was empty. "Damn." Outside, he approached two men in bib overalls and jackboots.

"Pardon me, gentlemen, could you tell me where I might find the marshal?"

"Over to the Ore House."

Not sure he understood, Tim asked, "The Ore House?"

"Yeah. Where all that music is comin' from. That's where he hangs out most of the time."

"Thanks." Tim went looking for the town marshal, but his mind was recalling more of White Shirt's words: the John Laws are interested only in their own welfare. If you want any justice, you'll have to do it yourself.

He wondered how much more he was going to have to do himself.

The marshal was easy to pick out of the crowd. He was standing at the bar among men in slouchy hats, pillbox caps, overalls, baggy wood pants, jackboots, and lace-up shoes. Men with calluses on their hands. But the marshal wore pants with a crease down the front, a gray vest with a gold-colored watch chain draped across the front, and a big silver star over his heart. He had a long handlebar moustache with waxed ends. And he had a pearl-handled pistol in a tooled leather holster high on his right hip.

Tim made his way through a crowd of drinkers. "Pardon me, sir, are you the marshal?"

The marshal put his beer mug on the bar. "Yessir. That's me."

"My name is Timothy Higgins. I'm with the HL cow outfit over in Parker County, and I've been following a herd of stolen cattle. I have reason to believe those cattle were loaded on railcars here six or seven days ago."

"Is that so? What happened to your head?"

Tim didn't answer, but said, "I'm hoping you saw them and asked who was shipping them and where they were going."

"No, son. I heard about some cattle being loaded at the railroad pens, but checking on cattle is the state's job, not mine."

"You say you're repping the HL?" The man asking wore blue jeans, riding boots and a curl-brim hat.

Tim turned to him and was pleased to recognize a fellow cattleman. "Yes sir."

"They were HL cattle, all right. I went and looked 'em over just out of curiosity. Feller said they come from over around Beutel in Johnson County. They'd been trailed a ways. You could see that."

"They'd been trailed a long ways. And I'll tell you something, something your sheriff ought to know." Tim told about the train robbery, the cattle cars, the spur line, and the sidetrack. When he finished, the marshal pulled on one end of his moustache and said:

"Well, I'll declare. You sure you know what you're

talking about, son?"

"You can see it yourself. The cars are still there, and the marks on the ground tell the story."

"I thought they were a shifty-eyed bunch," the rancher said.

"Did you learn anything about them? Who they were or anything?"

"Not much. Said they were going to market the cattle in Denver."

"What did they look like?"

"Purty hard to describe, except for a couple of 'em. One feller had a hook where his left hand used to be and another was a kid."

"Did they give any names?"

"No. They didn't act too friendly, and I didn't ask too many questions."

"Was one of them short and heavy with a round face?"

The rancher frowned at the floor a moment. "Yeah. I recollect one of 'em looked somethin' like that."

Tim looked at the marshal, hoping the lawman would have something to say. He looked next at the rancher. The rancher spoke again.

"Listen, young feller, they can't sell cattle without the brand being looked at and the owner checked. There ain't no brand inspector here, but there is in Denver. The brand inspectors work for the state, and they're s'posed to look at every brand in the stockyards. Now, them beefs were shipped to Denver, and the brand inspector there ought to know somethin' about 'em."

"Yeah," the marshal put in. "Checking brands is the state's job."

"Uh-huh." Tim shrugged his shoulders with resignation. "I guess I'm going to have to go to Denver."

It was a weary young cowboy who put his gray horse inside a box stall at the livery barn, saw that the horse had plenty of good green hay and a quarter gallon of oats. After counting his money he decided on a second-rate hotel, but one with hot water and a water closet where he could bathe and shave. Looking halfway civilized again, he ate a steak with mashed potatoes in a workingman's cafe, counted his money again, and decided to ride his horse to Denver instead of taking the train.

He let out a long sigh when he climbed into bed, a soft bed with enough blankets to keep anybody warm. But he didn't go to sleep right away.

Instead, he lay awake thinking about all that had happened, and wondering what was ahead. He'd shot it out with cattle rustlers and lost. Now he'd have to deal with government honchos and lawmen, and he wondered whether he'd do any better. As old White Shirt had often said:

Never trust anybody who works for the government.

Chapter Seventeen

It was street noise that woke him up, something he hadn't heard much of lately. Heavy freight wagons creaked down the street in front of the hotel, with trace chains and singletrees rattling. Teamsters yelled at the horses, careful not to use foul language in town where they would be heard by women and children.

Tim was reluctant to leave his warm bed, but he had enough money left to buy a good breakfast, and he was looking forward to that. He picked the same cafe where he'd had supper because it seemed to cater to the working class. Inside, he sat on a stool at a long counter and ordered ham and eggs and pancakes and coffee. He'd almost forgotten how good real food tasted, and he ate like a starving man. The coffee was especially good. He had three cups.

"What happened to your head?" The waitress was in her late teens and slender. She would have been pretty if she'd had proper dental care. When she smiled, as she was doing now, her crooked teeth ruined the symmetry of her face.

"Oh, not much." Tim smiled back at her. "Just had a, uh, accident."

"Do you work on a ranch around here?"

"Naw. I'm from Parker County. I'm here looking for some cattle."

"We don't serve very many cowboys. Most of our customers are miners and railroaders."

Silently, Tim compared her in her long dress and white apron with Mary Jane McCeogh in her wool knickers. Mary Jane was much prettier. But this girl was friendly, and Tim decided that if he lived anywhere near Black Hawk he'd take her to a dance. Or something.

When he paid his bill and left she said, "Good-bye. Come back."

The sky had cleared and the sun was warm on his face as he walked to the livery barn. There, he was happy to see that his horse had been grained and watered. Robert Ripp chuckled. "I'm glad I sold that horse. He eats like an elephant."

Chuckling with him, Tim allowed, "He's been eating better than I have, but good hay is something he hasn't had for a while."

"Learn anything about them cattle?"

"Yeah. They were the ones I've been looking for. The thieves are no doubt in Denver now."

"You goin' horseback?"

"Uh-huh. Can't afford a rail ticket, and I'll need a horse when I get there. Those streetcars don't go everywhere."

"Don't think they go anywheres near the stock-

146

yards, and I'll bet that's where you're headed."

"Yep."

The road to Denver was well-traveled, with only three steep grades. It wound through the town of Black Hawk to Clear Creek and followed the creek for miles. There were places, however, where it left the creek and climbed long hills. On the hills, Tim passed wagons that were stopped to let the horses blow. And when he got closer to the big city, just before he rode out of the foothills, he passed a wagonload of tourists who had disembarked and were picking wildflowers. He waved at them. Pretty women in dresses made of fine cotton. They smiled and waved back. Their wagon was a long one, with a row of spring seats. The driver, a man with a black hat and a black moustache, looked bored.

Out of Clear Creek Canyon, onto the rolling country of eastern Colorado, he could see the city of Denver spread out to the horizon in all directions. By then it was late afternoon, and he turned his horse toward the northeast section of the city and the union stockyards.

He hoped to spend the night at Aunt Josephine's house, but on the small chance that the stolen HL cattle were still in the stockyards, he wanted to waste no time getting there.

As tired as old Spook was, the first time he saw an electric streetcar he almost went through himself turning around and going the other way. Tim reined him up, chuckling. "I don't blame you. If I didn't know what it was, it'd scare hell out of me, too."

Passengers in the streetcar laughed at the horse's

antics, and the conductor clanged the bell again just to see what would happen. Tim controlled the horse easily and rode on. Old Spook had his head up and his ears twitching, leery of the sights, smells, and noise of the big city.

At the stockyards, Tim looked over fifteen acres of pens, some empty and some holding cattle, sheep, hogs, and even goats. The smell was so strong he tried to breathe without inhaling, found that impossible, and inhaled with short, quick gasps. Where to look?

The railroad cut through the middle of the pens, and on the other side were the slaughterhouses. The HL cattle, if not already slaughtered, were probably over there in the slaughterhouse pens. Tim turned his horse into a long alley between the pens, rode past a crew of cowboys sorting cattle, nodded at them, turned a corner, and rode down another alley. He crossed the railroad tracks, got down, and opened a wooden gate, led his horse through, shut the gate, mounted, and rode down still another alley.

A dozen pens held cattle of every breed and color. Tim rode past each pen, looking for the mixed breed of longhorns raised at the HL. He had to stop and stare at a man on horseback who rode up to a gate, reached down, unlatched it, rode his horse through and shut it without getting off his horse. The animal had been taught to sidestep around the end of an open gate.

"Evenin'," the man said.

"Good evening." Tim reined up next to him. "I'm looking for some cattle branded with the HL."

"The HL? Where did they come from?" The man hooked his right leg over the saddle horn and pulled a sack of tobacco from a shirt pocket.

"From over in Parker County."

"Where's that?" He rolled a smoke and struck a wooden match on the saddle horn.

"West and south. In the Gunnison Valley."

"Way over there, huh? Naw, I ain't seen that brand. But there's a lot of cattle come through here I don't see."

"Is there anybody who does see all of them?"

"The state boys, the brand inspectors."

"Where can I find them?"

The man nodded in the direction of a two-story building on the south side of the stockyards. "They got an office over there. Doubt if they're there now. They're at home feedin' their faces."

Tim looked at the sky. The sun sat on top of a mountain to the west. He'd forgotten how late in the day it was. "Oh. Yeah. Well, I guess they don't work at night."

"Huh," the man snorted. "Not the government boys. Stock has to be fed and loaded and unloaded at all hours of the day and night, but them government boys know when it's quittin' time."

"Could anybody move a herd of cattle through here at night without the brand inspectors seeing them?"

"Naw. That'd be agin the law. Somebody'd see 'em."

"Oh. Well, I guess I'll go over there just in case somebody's still around."

Finding his way to the building through the alleys, between the pens, and around the corners was like working a puzzle, but Tim managed it. The building was locked.

"Well, hell, old feller," Tim said to the gray horse, "let's go see Aunt Josie. I hope there's some hay in that

149

stable out back. And won't she be surprised to see me again."

Traffic—horse-drawn buggies and wagons and a few bicycles—had thinned out now that it was suppertime. Tim found his way to West Colfax and rode east to Broadway and then to Pearl Street. At his aunt's house he dismounted and tied his horse to a ring in a hitching post, then walked stiff-legged onto the wooden porch.

Mrs. Josephine Webber had been looking out the window at the street, and she saw him coming. She opened the door just as he reached for it.

"Timothy, for heaven's sake. What happened? You look terrible."

He grinned a crooked grin. "You should have seen me yesterday, Aunt Josie. I've shaved and had a couple of good meals since then."

She hugged him and kissed him on the cheek, then stepped back and looked him over carefully. "What have you been living on? You look starved. I've never seen anyone so peak-ud. Come in this house."

"I've got a horse to take care of, Aunt Josie. Is there any hay in the stable out back?"

"I think there is. I haven't looked in there for weeks."

"I hope there is. If there isn't, I'll have to find some."

"Mr. Paulson next door will lend you some. He keeps a horse."

"Okay, I'll go take care of this one. He's carried me a long ways and up a lot of mountains."

"You go feed your horse and then you come in here and I'll feed you."

There was hay. The last horseman to use the stable had left a six-foot pile of good prairie grass. Tim

150

pumped a bucket of water for his horse, filled a manger with the hay, and bid him goodnight.

In the house, Aunt Josephine fed him roast pork, boiled potatoes, homemade bread and apple butter, and a wedge of apple pie. He ate until he could hold no more. Then he told her everything that had happened.

"This should be reported, Timothy. You can't let them get by with this."

"I reported it to the town marshal at Central City, and you can bet he'll report it to the sheriff, and you can bet he'll make a big deal out of it. He wants to get reelected, and you can bet he'll take credit for finding those missing railroad cars."

"What are you going to do now?"

"Find out who stole those cattle. They were shipped to the Denver Union Stockyards, that's for sure, and somebody, a brand inspector, had to have seen them. They were shipped there to be sold, and whoever sold them had to have signed a bill of sale."

"What will you do when you find out who sold them?"

"Report them to the law. If I'm lucky, maybe I can get some of the money that was paid for them."

Aunt Josephine started gathering dirty dishes. "At least, if you find out who stole and sold those cattle, you can have them arrested so they can't steal anymore."

"Yeah." But that brought an unpleasant thought to Tim's mind: the one-handed Joseph Holt and his stepdaughter, Ellen. They had saved his life. He stood and scraped his plate. "What I'd rather do is get the money for them."

*　　　*　　　*

For a while next morning, Tim couldn't go anywhere. While he slept his Aunt Josephine had stolen his clothes, scrubbed them clean on a corrugated washboard, and hung them on a line in the backyard to dry.

"Say," Tim complained, "what do you think I'm gonna wear?"

"You can wear some of your late uncle's clothes around the house, and you don't need to go anywhere right now, anyway. You need more rest."

He put on a pair of bib overalls that were four sizes too big in the waist and went out and took care of his horse. He stuffed himself again with pancakes and eggs, and was restless. "Maybe I can put them on wet and let them dry on me."

"And catch your death of pneumonia?"

He waited. About midmorning he took his clothes from the line and put them on. The jeans were damp around the pockets. Old Spook blinked in the sunlight when Tim led him from the stable. "You won't have to go far today, old feller."

Before he left, his aunt handed him two peanut butter and jelly sandwiches wrapped in a denim jacket and insisted that he be back for supper. "If you aren't back, I'm going to have the police looking for you."

"I'll be back. And I think I'll know more about what happened to those beeves and who stole them."

But as he rode away, to East Colfax and then west toward the stockyards, he wasn't so sure. He had tracked the cattle as far as he could, and now he would have to depend on government officials and officers of the law. Again, his dad's words came to him:

You can't trust nobody in government.

Chapter Eighteen

He went first to the stockyards administration building and asked for the brand inspector. An office with a dirty glass pane was pointed out to him. He knocked on the door and waited for an answer.

"Yeah."

He opened the door and looked in. A pudgy man with thick gray hair, a gray moustache, and long gray sideburns sat at a rolltop desk littered with papers. A hand-painted sign on his desk identified him as William Garrison, Brand Inspector, State of Colorado.

"Yeah?"

"Are you the brand inspector?"

"That I am." The man leaned back in a spring-backed swivel chair.

"Mr. Garrison, my name is Timothy Higgins. My father owns the HL outfit in Parker County, and I'm looking for some stolen HL cattle that I believe were brought here."

"Yeah? Stolen?"

"Yes, sir."

"What makes you think they were brought here?" The brand inspector was looking hard at him.

"I tracked them as far as Black Hawk, sir, and I was told that some cattle wearing that brand were loaded on railcars there. They had to have come here."

"That's not necessarily so. They could have gone on to Omaha. A lot of cattle are shipped from here to Omaha."

Tim shuffled his feet. The brand inspector's hard stare made him feel inferior in some way. He stammered, "Uh, sir, do you . . . do you check the brands of cattle that come through here on the way to Omaha?"

"We don't if they're not unloaded. And if they were loaded at Black Hawk, they could have gone right on out of the state."

Suddenly, Tim felt defeated. For the first time since he'd left the HL, he felt all hope drain out of him. He couldn't go to Omaha. In the first place he didn't have the train fare, and in the second place the cattle would have been slaughtered and forgotten about. And in the third place he didn't know anything about branding laws in Nebraska. For that matter, he didn't know very much about branding laws in Colorado. He felt like just turning around and walking out. He shuffled his feet again. He decided to try one more question.

"Sir, did you see any cattle branded with an HL?"

"Nope. Not me."

Tim swallowed a lump in his throat. He tasted defeat. But William Garrison's answer led to another question. "Well, is there more than one brand inspector here?"

"Yeah, there's Walt."

154

"Walt? Where can I find him?"

"He's out of town."

"When will he be back?"

"No telling."

"Can I wait?"

William Garrison shrugged. "It's a free country. But you can't wait in here. I've got paperwork to do. You people have no idea how much paperwork goes with a government job. Everything we do has to go on paper." He put his elbows on the desk and stared at the top of it. "Paper, paper, paper."

That brought another question to Tim's mind. "Does Walt, uh, put everything on paper?"

Garrison's head swiveled around. "Yep. But if you're thinking what I think you're thinking, you can't."

Tim digested that. He remembered another one of White Shirt's comments about government officials: "Everything is supposed to be above board. Everything is supposed to be public record. But they'll let you see what they want you to see and nothin' else. Unless you hand 'em some money. Or haul off and knock 'em on their asses. Personally, I'd rather kick the hound dog shit out of 'em."

Frustration burned into Tim's mind. The frustration of spending too many nights with too little to eat and not enough clothes to keep him warm, of being shot, and of tracking the cattle all the way from the Gunnison Valley to Denver only to be stymied by a government fathead. He felt like walking up to William Garrison and punching him. He was standing on the man's left. A left hook to the nose ought to straighten him up and a right cross to the jaw ought to knock him down. Tim clenched his fists. I ought to do it, he told himself. I ought to knock him on his government ass.

But—he forced himself to relax—what good would it do? None. It wouldn't help him find out what had happened to the HL cattle. But dammit.

"Listen, Mr. Garrison, I'm trying to find some stolen cattle. You are paid by the state to check the brands of every cow brute that comes through here. I want to know whether you've seen the HL brand. If you don't want to cooperate with me, I'll find out who your boss is and go see him."

"Are you threatening me, young feller?"

Tim had had enough. "You're damn right, I am. You do your job or I'll raise more hell than you can stand."

Garrison jumped to his feet. "See here, young feller, you can't talk to me like that. Get out of here."

Hands on hips, feet apart, Tim stared at the end of the man's nose. He spoke through his teeth. "Try to throw me out."

"Feisty little rooster, aren't you. Well, by God, I don't have to take this kind of shit from anyone." He took two steps toward Tim. Stopped. Tom stood fast, fists clenched, ready.

"Mornin', Bill. Or maybe it's afternoon." The voice came from behind Tim. Tim spun on his heels.

"Thought I'd drop by and see if Walt got off all right."

"Uh, yes sir, Ted." Garrison's face had gone soft. "He left this morning on the Denver and Santa Fe. He's in Colorado Springs by now."

"Walt?" Tim interrupted. "The brand inspector?"

"And who might you be?" The newcomer was a portly man in a wrinkled business suit with a red necktie. His fedora hat was shoved back on his head, allowing a sheaf of brown hair to fall across his forehead.

Garrison answered. "This is some smart kid that's trying to tell me how to do my job."

"And why would you do that, young man?" He was looking Tim over from the spurs on his boots to the bandage on his head. But his expression was friendly.

"Sir," Tim exhaled audibly, "I'm trying to find out what happened to some cattle stolen about a month ago from the HL outfit in Parker County. I believe they came through here."

"Stolen, huh? How many cattle are you talking about?"

"A hundred head of prime beeves. Give or take a few."

"The HL, huh?" The fat man walked over to the rolltop desk, took a pair of wire-rimmed reading glasses from a breast pocket, put them on, and rummaged through a drawer. He pulled out a clipboard with a sheaf of papers attached to it. "Seems to me I did hear something about the HL brand."

"Ted," Garrison put in, "Walt probably took his papers with him."

"Umm. Let's see." The man named Ted was turning pages. "No, here's something. Hmm." He looked over at Tim. "Did you say they came from Parker County?"

"Yes, sir."

"This bunch came from Gilpin County. Branded with an HL on the left hip. An underslope in the left ear."

Now Tim had hope. "That's my dad's brand. He earmarks his cattle with an underbit on the left ear, but that could be changed easy to an underslope."

"How many did you say?"

"About a hundred."

"A hundred and three. All dry stuff. Steers and heifers. What did you say your name is?"

"Higgins. Timothy Higgins. My dad is John Higgins."

"Hmm. Nope. These cattle were sold by a, uh, let's see, a Benjamin Jones of Gilpin County."

Excitement was building in Tim now. He was getting somewhere. "No, sir," he almost shouted. "Benjamin Jones is a thief. He's one of the bunch that stole those cattle. He stole two horses of mine, too."

"Well now, just a doggone minute, son. This whole thing got the approval of Walt, and he knows what he's doing."

For a moment, Tim didn't know what to say. A hard knot began forming in his stomach. A few seconds ago he had thought he was close to the answer, but now he was confused again. "Walt?" he said in a strangled voice. "The brand inspector?"

"Yeah. Walt Blessing."

"How . . . how many are there?"

"Quite a few. We have to be practically everywhere."

"And Walt Blessing is the one that's out of town?"

"Yep. He's on his way to Pueblo. They ship a lot of cattle out of Pueblo."

"Well, uh . . ." Tim was trying to think. "Uh, how, uh, what makes him think the cattle belonged to somebody named Benjamin Jones? I mean, uh, aren't the brands registered with the Secretary of State?"

"Good question, son." The fat man put the clipboard on the desk and opened another drawer. "Got a book here somewhere." He rummaged through that drawer

158

and pulled out a foot-square ledger. "Let's see, umm." He read, turned pages. "Yep. It's right here. The HL is registered to Benjamin Jones."

"Huh?" Tim couldn't believe it. "It can't be."

"It's right here, son. Look for yourself."

He handed the book to Tim, opened. Tim looked at the page. It contained a drawing of a steer and showed the brand and its location on the steer. It also contained the name, mailing address and grazing range of the owner. Tim's heart dropped into his stomach. The name was Benjamin Jones of Gilpin County.

All he could do was sputter. "But . . . but . . . it can't be. Somebody's made a mistake. My dad owns the HL brand." He turned pages, hoping to find another HL brand. Or something. The pages were loose, held with ring binders.

"Did he get it registered proper?"

"Of course, he did."

"All I know is what I see here in the book."

"Well, uh, how come the pages are loose?"

An exasperated sigh came from the fat man. "Ranches are bought and sold all the time, and the brands go with them. We have to keep up."

"Who makes the changes? The Secretary of State?"

"That's right."

Tim felt like a man who had just been hit on the head with a singletree. His mind was numb.

"Well, I got to get on out in the yard. Got work to do. Bill, you coming?"

"Yeah." Garrison stood and went to the door. "Got to lock up, kid. That means you havta get your ass out."

Feeling dazed, Tim went out into the sunlight. He

untied his horse from the hitchrail, mounted. Where to go next? He had to think this over. He had to figure this out.

He was waiting for a streetcar to pass at Seventeenth and Arapahoe when he heard his name called. His gray horse was fidgeting at the screeching sound of the streetcar.

"Timothy." It was a female voice. Not his Aunt Josephine. "Timothy."

Looking back on Arapahoe he saw her waving frantically to get his attention. A pretty dark-haired girl in a pretty print dress that came down to her black patent leather slippers. "Timothy."

"Well, for . . ." He reined his horse around toward her. The girl was smiling from ear to ear.

"Timothy. How wonderful to see you."

He dismounted. "Mary Jane. It's good to see you, too." He held out his hand to shake.

But she didn't shake his hand. Instead she stepped close, put her arms around his waist and hugged him. Pedestrians on the busy sidewalk had to step around him and his horse. He was embarrassed at the public display of affection.

Stepping back, she looked into his eyes, still smiling. "What are you doing in the city? Never mind, I'm just so happy to see you again. How are you?"

"Why, I'm fine, Mary Jane. How are you? Did you finally get enough to eat? Did you finally get warm? You sure are pretty."

"You're looking better, too. Except for that awful bandage on your head. Did you really get shot?"

Grinning, he said, "Yeah, but that's a long story."

"Did you find your cattle?"

He shook his head and his smile slipped. "No. Not yet. They were brought here, but . . ." He shrugged.

"Well, you must tell me all about it. I was just going into the tea shop at Daniels and Fisher. Can you tie your horse and come in?"

Looking down at himself, he was embarrassed again. "I, uh, I'm really not dressed for that place."

"But we must visit. Come to the house tonight. I'd like you to meet my mother, and she certainly wants to meet you. I told her all about you."

"Tonight? Well, sure. Uh, what time?"

"Come for dinner. At seven. We'd love to have you."

"Dinner? Uh, Mary Jane, I just came down from the hills and the clothes I'm wearing are all I have with me. I'm sorry, I . . ."

"Perfectly all right. I understand, and my mother will understand. We're not snobs, Timothy. If you don't come I'll be terribly disappointed. Incidentally, where are you staying?"

"With an aunt. A widow. My mother's sister."

"Oh, yes, you told me about her."

At that moment, Tim was chastised. Not by the girl but by two matronly pedestrians who had to walk around the horse. "Young man. That animal does not belong on the sidewalk. If you do not remove it at once I shall call a policeman."

"Oh, excuse me, ma'am. I'll move him."

The girl giggled, then frowned. "She doesn't know it, Timothy, but that horse was a life saver. I had walked as far as I could when you and that horse came along." She reached out and scratched the horse on the neck.

"How are you, Spook? It's good to see you, too."

To Timothy she said, "Do you have the piece of paper I wrote my address on?"

"Yeah." He reached into his shirt pocket. "Here it is."

"We'll expect you at seven, then?"

"Yeah, sure, okay."

She left, walking toward Sixteenth Street, her back straight and her long dress pulled in at the middle showing off her hourglass figure. Tim shook his head and grinned a wry grin. "Ain't she something?"

He was glad to find his aunt wasn't at home. Out grocer shopping, probably. He realized with chagrin that he couldn't pay her for his board right now. But he knew she would trust him to pay her later. She might even refuse payment.

"Now's my chance," he said to himself, "to do something I've been dreading, but have to do. If Aunt Josie were here she'd insist I go to a doctor."

He borrowed his late uncle's straight razor and strop, and he borrowed his aunt's eyebrow tweezers, and he propped a mirror on the windowsill over the kitchen sink—where the light was good—and started.

First he pulled off the bandage. "Oooh," he grunted. "Should have done this sooner, before the hair started growing back." He pulled it a little at a time, then squinched his eyes shut and ripped it off. "Gawd."

Next he sharpened the razor on the leather strop, and then, carefully, holding his breath, cut one of the catgut stitches on the side of his head. That didn't

162

hurt. But now came the painful part. Using the tweezers, he took hold of one end of the stitch and pulled it out. That stung.

"Gawd."

He cut and pulled out another. Then another. His eyes watered from the pain and he had to stop for a moment and wipe his eyes with his shirt sleeve. Then another. And another.

When he finished, the wound was bleeding, and he washed it with water from the kitchen pump. Next he poured out a palmful of his late uncle's Bay Rum aftershave lotion and daubed it on the wound. The alcohol in the lotion stung and made his eyes water again, but he believed it would prevent infection. That done, he looked through cabinets until he found his aunt's first aid kit in a white tin box with a red cross on it, and he fashioned himself a clean bandage. Then he grinned at himself in the mirror.

"Won't show a couple of weeks from now. The hair will grow over it. You aren't such a handsome sonofabuck, anyhow."

His aunt would notice the clean bandage and she would ask questions, but the deed was done and she was smart enough not to dwell on the subject. He had other things to think about. Like how badly he had conducted himself in the brand inspector's office. Hadn't used his head at all. Ready to fight. Wouldn't that have been smart? Could've been thrown in jail. Could've got his head hurt again. Wouldn't have learned anything.

What had he learned?

It was obvious, now that he was thinking about it:

163

somebody is a crook. Either a brand inspector named Walt Blessing, or somebody in the Secretary of State's office. No two men can register the same brand. Not unless somebody made a bad mistake. And that wasn't likely. What to do about it?

Now, there was a question.

Chapter Nineteen

He had guessed right about his aunt. She scolded him for taking the stitches out of his wound, and she tried to talk him into letting a doctor look at it, but when she realized he had his mind set, she let the matter drop. And when he told her he was having dinner with a girl, she brightened and smiled.

"Why, Timothy. How nice. I was hoping you'd meet a nice girl in Denver. What does her father do?"

"He's, uh, she told me, what was it? Oh yeah, he's an Indian agent. Buys groceries for the Indians on the reservation. The Utes, I guess."

"Then he works for the U.S. Government. That's a good job. Maybe he could put in the right words for you, Timothy, and you could get a job with the U.S. Government."

Tim grinned. "Wouldn't John have a conniption? He hates the government."

"We have to have a government. Why, without a government we'd all be living like savages."

165

"Yeah. Can't argue about that."

The house on Washington Street was Victorian, painted white. Big, and recently built. It was in a block of big houses. Expensive. How, Tim wondered as he walked up the path through a broad green lawn, can an Indian agent afford a house like this?

Mary Jane met him at the door and ushered him inside. He looked at the oak furniture, the brocaded draperies, the plush carpet, the spiral staircase, and the moss rock fireplace, and he looked down at himself. He wished he hadn't come.

Mrs. McCeogh was a tall, slender woman who walked with a stiff back and had a dignified air about her. But she smiled a nice smile and held out her hand. "How nice to meet you, Mr. Higgins. I have heard so much about you. I will always be grateful to you for rescuing Mary Jane."

Again he was aware of his faded jeans, plain shirt, and scuffed boots. He took Mrs. McCeogh's hand gently, afraid he'd crush it. She took him by the arm and steered him toward an overstuffed leather chair.

"Mr. McCeogh likes a snifter of whiskey before dinner, Mr. Higgins, would you care for some bourbon? Or perhaps some scotch?"

"No thank you, ma'am. I'm not quite old enough to drink legally, and I don't really care for whiskey, anyhow." Was he mistaken or did he see approval on Mrs. McCeogh's face?

"Father isn't here tonight, Timothy. He's away on business. It will be just the three of us for dinner."

"He will be disappointed that he missed you, Mr.

Higgins. He spoke well of you, and he regrets that you refused his offer of a, uh, reimbursement, shall we say?"

"It wasn't much. A few cans of airtights."

"Pardon me, a few cans of . . . ?"

"Airtights. That's what some folks call canned food."

"Oh, I see."

Mary Jane wrinkled her nose. "It's the most bland food you can imagine, Mother, but it's easy to carry and it's nourishment. And I was desperately in need of some nourishment."

Mrs. McCeogh chuckled a good-natured chuckle. "I daresay we shall dine better than that tonight? Would you care for a cigar, Mr. Higgins?"

"No, ma'am. Thank you just the same."

A black maid served dinner. It began with a thick soup that Tim couldn't identify, but it was delicious. The main course was breaded pork chops and that was followed by a cake with thick, sweet icing. After dinner they returned to the drawing room.

"Would you like a wee bit of brandy, Mr. Higgins?"

"Thank you, ma'am, but I'm not used to drinking liquor at all." He sat in the same leather chair.

"Tell me about your ranch, Mr. Higgins. Mary Jane said your family owns one of the largest ranches in Colorado."

"It's the HL, Mrs. McCeogh. Yes, I think it is one of the biggest. My dad and his dad drove a herd of Texas longhorns to the Gunnison Valley about thirty years ago and settled there. My grandfather died before I was born."

"How interesting. Your father is a real pioneer, then."

Tim grinned. "Yes, he is. The land belonged to the Utes then, and they were mostly friendly, but my dad and granddad had to fight off the Cheyenne who sometimes drifted over that way. They bought the land from the Utes. They paid for it with hard-earned money, but now the government isn't sure the sale was legal."

Mrs. McCeogh's face registered disappointment. "Then the ownership of the land is in question?"

"Some of it. My dad bought title to a lot of land from the government and has a deed to prove it."

"Oh." She was relieved. "Tell me, why did your family settle way out there?"

Tim shrugged. "The land was available. The Indians were mostly friendly. And," he grinned, "as my dad tells it, he asked the Indians where they killed the fattest buffalo, and he settled where they pointed. It's good grassland."

"How very interesting. And you are your father's only heir?"

That brought a frown to Tim's face, but he quickly forced himself to smile. "Yes. That I am."

"But," Mary Jane put in, "Timothy's thinking about settling in Denver, aren't you, Timothy?"

"I, uh, I've thought about it, yes."

Mrs. McCeogh asked about the stolen cattle, and Tim told her only part of the story. It was Mary Jane who told Mrs. McCeogh that the bandage on his head covered a bullet wound. Tim wished she hadn't done that.

"It was, uh, not much of a wound."

168

"But how did it happen, Mr. Higgins?"

"Well, uh, I got too close to the stolen cattle, and there were some shots fired and I got the worst of it. Lucky for me there was a doctor nearby."

"How terrible. Sometimes we in the city forget how untamed the rest of the state is. Even with the Indians confined to the reservations, it seems to be an extremely dangerous place. I sometimes worry about Mr. McCeogh when he visits the reservations. Is there no law out there?"

"Oh yes, there is. But," Tim smiled again, "it's not like the city where there's a cop on every corner."

"I see." Mrs. McCeogh stood. "Well, I'll leave you young people to visit." She excused herself politely and left the room.

"Would you like to go for a walk, Timothy? It's a lovely evening."

"Sure, okay."

She hugged his arm as they walked slowly down Washington Street toward the electric lights on Colfax. They talked about unimportant matters. She was all softly feminine, and he was very much aware of that. Her hand on his arm made his knees weak. And when she stopped and turned to him, facing him close, he thought his knees were going to buckle.

"Timothy, would you like to kiss me?"

"Huh?" He couldn't believe it. "Here? Now?"

"Like this." She took his face in both hands, pulled his head down, and kissed him soundly on the mouth.

"But . . ."

She kissed him again. This time he returned the kiss and thought he was going to collapse. It was like nothing he had ever experienced before. So soft, so . . .

When she stepped back, finally, she smiled. "Will you come to see me again, Timothy?"

"Uh, sure, you bet."

"Promise?"

"Promise."

"Well then, walk me back."

In the front yard at her house, she pulled him into a shadow and kissed him again. "Don't forget." And she walked briskly to the door and went inside.

On his way back to Pearl Street, Tim couldn't believe what had happened. She was the prettiest girl he had ever seen. Beautiful. Smart. The kind of girl young men dream about.

"Damn," he said to himself. "I think I'm in love."

While Tim was trying to decide what to do next, a newspaper decided for him.

It was a story in the *Rocky Mountain News* that caught his eye when his Aunt Josephine brought the paper in from the street the next morning. The front page headline read:

GIRL NABBED AFTER SHOOTING

The story read:

"Gunfire erupted on Larimer Street in downtown Denver Tuesday, resulting in the arrest of a man and a girl. The girl was at first believed to be a boy.

"Witnesses said four persons were involved in the shooting, but apparently there were no injuries. Two men traded shots with the arrested pair in the lobby of the Great Northern Hotel and ran down an alley where they eluded police, witnesses said.

"The pair arrested refused to identify themselves or give any statement to police. They were registered in the hotel as Robert Burford and Clarence Burford of Grand Junction. The man is minus his left hand and wears a hook on his left wrist. He would say only that the shooting was a personal matter. Police said he apparently fired two shots from a large caliber revolver. The girl was holding a revolver when police arrived, but it was not determined whether she had fired it.

"The two were arrested when police converged on the hotel and cornered them in the lobby."

Aunt Josephine interrupted Tim's reading. "Aren't you coming to breakfast, Timothy?"

"Huh? Oh, yeah. Just a minute." He read on.

"The man and girl were believed at first to be father and son, even though they had occupied separate rooms at the hotel. The girl was dressed in denim trousers and a man's shirt, and was not identified as female until she was searched at the Denver city jail.

"A witness said the pair was in the hotel lobby when the other two men came in from the street. An argument ensued, and then the shooting began. It is believed four shots were fired, and police say it is miraculous that no one was injured."

"Timothy." Aunt Josephine was growing impatient. "Your hotcakes are getting cold."

"Oh, uh, sure. I'm coming." His mind was spinning again. The pair had to be Joe Holt and his stepdaughter, Ellen Olsen. In a gunfight. Why? A disagreement with his fellow rustlers? And Ellen. Did she use a gun? Had she had a gun when she took him to a doctor up there at

Rosebud? He couldn't remember. Not Ellen. Not that little girl in the homemade coat who couldn't keep her stockings up.

"Put some syrup on your hotcakes, Timothy."

"Huh? Oh, sure."

"Where is your mind this morning? On that girl you visited last night? By the way, how was the visit? Was her mother nice?"

"Yeah. Real nice. Nice folks."

They're in jail. That's no place for Ellen Olsen. Her mother is a lady. Not enough money, but a polite and pleasant woman. How could little Ellen end up in jail? There's something crazy about this whole damn thing.

"Well, she certainly has your mind occupied." Aunt Josephine got up and poured more coffee. "What are your plans for today, Timothy?"

"Oh, uh, I don't know. I think I'll, uh, go over to the state capitol and see the Secretary of State. There's a mixup over the HL brand."

He had to go see her. See if he could do anything for her. "Uh, Aunt Josie, where is the city jail?"

"The city jail? Why, it's on Bannock Street, I think. Beyond the capitol. Why, Timothy?"

"I just read in the paper that some people were arrested yesterday who might have something to do with John's cattle."

The walk to the city jail was a short one. A few blocks downhill to Broadway and across busy Broadway to Bannock, and there was the city and county building. Tim stood in front of the city hall, saw a sign that said the police department was in back, and walked around

172

the building. It was a two-story brick. A uniformed officer with a billy club hanging from his belt on the left and a pistol in a holster on the right was sitting at a desk. Behind the officer was a steel door. "Pardon me," Tim said, unsure of himself, "I wonder if I might visit with one of the prisoners."

"Who? And why?" The officer stood, and he had to have been at least six-three. His soup-strainer moustache almost covered his mouth.

Tim felt small and insignificant in front of the officer, and for a moment he didn't answer. He was trying to make up his mind about something that had been worrying him during his walk to the jail. Finally he said, "Sir, I'd like to tell you something. It's something to do with a crime in Parker County and Gilpin County and possibly in Denver."

The officer eyed him with suspicion. "What?"

"Uh, sir, my name is Timothy Higgins. My father, John Higgins, owns the HL Ranch in Parker County. I have trailed a hundred cattle that were stolen from the ranch as far as Denver. I believe a man named Benjamin Jones is one of the thieves. I believe he . . ."

The officer interrupted, "Parker County? Where's that?"

"It's in the Gunnison Valley, sir. The county seat is Shiprock."

"Yeah, so what about this Benjamin Jones?"

"Well, sir, in the first place he also stole two horses from me, and I found one of them in Black Hawk, where it was sold by Benjamin Jones. And the cattle were loaded in railcars at Black Hawk and shipped to Denver. A man named Benjamin Jones claimed ownership."

"Gilpin County, huh?"

"Yes, sir."

"So what's that got to do with a prisoner in this jail? We ain't got no Benjamin Jones locked up."

"I believe two of your prisoners know Benjamin Jones."

"And who might they be?"

"The Burfords."

"Oh, them. Well, what do you want to see them for?"

"They might tell me something about Benjamin Jones and where I can find him."

The officer's eyes narrowed. "Do you know what you're talking about, young feller? And what happened to your head?"

"Yes, sir, I know what I'm talking about. Can you wire the sheriff in Gilpin County? I'll bet he's found three stolen railcars by now. Two cattle cars and a waycar. They were stolen by the same gang that stole my dad's cattle and my horses."

"Wal, now." The officer rubbed his jaw. "I don't know about that. Where is your dad?"

"He's at home. He sent me to find the cattle."

"He sent a kid?"

"Yes, sir."

"Wal, I don't know. I'll have to talk to the chief about that."

"Will you do that, sir? I'll bet the sheriff at Black Hawk would like to find Benjamin Jones."

"Wal, I'll talk to the chief when he gets here. He ain't here right now."

"Can I see one of the prisoners?"

"Which one?"

"The girl, uh, whatever her name is."

"Why her?"

"I think I might know her."

"Oh, you do, huh? Wal, we'd like to know more about her. Her and her old man."

"Is there a bail?"

"Not yet. The judge ain't seen 'em yet, and he's the one sets bail."

"Can I see her?"

The officer thought it over. "You ain't a beau or somethin', are you?"

"No sir. I'm not even sure I know her."

"Wal, I reckon it'll be all right." He opened a drawer in the desk, took out a large key ring with a half-dozen big keys on it and unlocked the door behind him.

Tim followed him through the door, down a corridor of jail cells, four of them occupied by men, and around a corner, where the officer unlocked another door. He saw the girl, then. She was sitting on a steel bunk, looking down at the floor, paying no attention to the two men who stopped in front of her cell.

"Ellen?"

She looked up and her eyes widened. But she didn't move.

"Uh, officer, can I talk to her alone?"

"Do you know her?"

"Yes sir, I do."

After a moment's hesitation, the officer said, "Wal, all right, but only for a minute. And I gotta shake you down first. Wouldn't do for you to slip her a gun or anything."

Tim stood with his arms out while the officer ran his hands over his body, down his legs, up his crotch and under his armpits. He took off his hat so the officer

175

could inspect that.

"Only for a minute." The officer left.

"Ellen?" Still, she didn't move.

"Ellen, what happened? Can I help you? I owe you, you know."

She looked up, then. "Timothy, will you please go away? You can't help me."

"I will if I can, Ellen."

She stood. Her dress was plain gray cotton. A jail dress. She wore riding boots, probably because the jail didn't have anything else to put on her feet. Her hair was short and parted on the side. "I'm happy to see you recovered, Timothy. But you should go home. Whatever happens to me, I deserve it."

"You were a good kid once, Ellen."

"I'm a thief."

"I'm gonna get you out of here."

"You can't."

"I will. Where's Joe?"

"I think he's in a cell around the corner."

"I'm gonna get you both out."

"How?"

"I'll pay your bail."

"They haven't set bail."

"Then I'll bust you out."

Chapter Twenty

Bust her out, sure, Tim mumbled to himself as he walked to his aunt's house. Just how in holy hell am I gonna do that? Hell, I haven't even got a gun. Or have I? That old Army Colt Uncle Wilbur had is still in the house somewhere. No ammunition for it. Probably can't even buy ammunition for a cap and ball pistol anymore. But it's a big sonofagun and it might scare hell out of somebody. If I can sneak it out of the house without Aunt Josie knowing about it.

He pumped another bucket of water for his horse and led the horse up and down the alley a couple of times to keep its legs limber. "You need some rest anyhow, old feller." He kept an eye on the house, hoping his aunt would go out, go to the grocery store or go visit the neighbors or something. At noon, she hadn't left the house.

There were other things he ought to be doing. Like going to the Secretary of State's office and trying to find out how two men registered the same brand. And, just out of curiosity, go back to the stockyards and try to find out who bought those cattle. Whoever it was— probably one of the packing houses—would claim the cattle were bought in good faith from a man who was the registered owner and they had committed no crime. They wouldn't give a dime to the rightful owner. Not even if he could prove he was the rightful owner. A lawyer might get something out of them, but he didn't have time for lawyers.

The last thing he should be doing was committing a crime himself. Joe Holt and Ellen Olsen had gotten themselves into that pickle. He ought to leave them in jail.

But they had saved his life. She had, anyhow, and he had helped. She couldn't have done it if he hadn't talked the rest of the bunch into leaving her behind up there near Rosebud.

Besides, he had to find Benjamin Jones. Joe Holt and Ellen Olsen ought to know where to find him.

Come on, Aunt Josie, go for a walk or something. I've got to get this done tonight.

It was midafternoon when Aunt Josephine left the house. "I'm going to the grocery store, Timothy. I'll be back in an hour or so."

"All right. I think I'll stick around here the rest of the day." He quickly made up a lie. "I'm gonna go see Mary Jane McCeogh tonight."

Now was his chance. He went into her bedroom and rummaged through the dresser drawer. Lots of silky underclothes and embroidered handkerchiefs, but no gun. He searched a closet and found the gun in a shoebox on the top shelf. Feeling guilty about prowling through his aunt's belongings, he took the gun and carried it out to the stable.

It was a heavy gun with a once blued barrel now shiny with wear. Inside the stable, he held it in his right hand, in a shooting position. Good balance. The walnut grips fit his hand perfectly. "Wish I had the stuff it takes to load it," he said to himself. "I'll bet it's fun to shoot." He chuckled when he recalled a cowboy's comments about an old cap and ball rifle. If too much powder was poured in, the gun shot flames and smoke as well as a lead ball. "And," the cowboy joked, "it'll cook your meat as well as kill it."

As an afterthought, he went back into the house, found some of his uncle's overalls and a railroader's cap and took them out to the stable, too. Then he snapped his fingers, hurried back inside, borrowed a long heavy denim jacket and grabbed the bandana the girl had left for him at Rosebud.

At supper he was quiet. He just didn't feel like talking. His aunt tried to get him to talk about Mary Jane McCeogh, but got nothing but short answers to her questions.

"Well, anyway, I think it's nice that you're seeing a nice girl. And I'll bet her father could help you get a job with the U.S. Government. I only wish you had better clothes. Can't you buy more clothes, Timothy?"

"Naw. Not until I find a job or until I get the money for John's cattle. He'll owe me ninety-seven dollars, the money I spent out of my own pocket."

"It's too bad you had to spend your own money."

"Yeah, The only way I'll get it back is to get the money for those beeves."

Just after dark, he combed his hair, wiped his boots, and left. "I don't know when I'll be back. Don't wait up for me."

179

"Now you be nice to that girl, Timothy."

He walked to the end of the block, then doubled back down the alley to the stable. The horse snorted at him when he groped his way inside and changed into his late uncle's clothes. The clothes were baggy and the pockets were big, but they wouldn't hold the heavy gun. He solved the problem by taking the belt from his own pants, cinching it around his waist and carrying the gun inside it. He had to tighten it to hold the gun in place. His skinning knife was still hanging from the belt. The long jacket concealed it all nicely.

It seemed like a long walk to Bannock Street, and when he passed under the electric lights on Broadway he was afraid he'd look suspicious in the oversized clothes. Pedestrian traffic was light, and no one paid him any attention.

Outside the entrance to the police department, he stopped, tried to relax and mentally prepare himself. What he was doing was crazy. What if there was a bunch of cops inside? He couldn't handle more than one or two. And what if they put up a fight? He didn't want to shoot anybody. Hell, he couldn't shoot anybody with an unloaded gun. He could be stopped cold and put in jail himself. He could be shot and killed.

Give it up, his mind told him. This is a crazy damnfool thing to do. But when he looked at it that way, everything he'd done in the past couple of weeks was crazy. He'd been taking chances ever since he left the HL.

He took the bandana out of his hip pocket and tied it around his face, then took the gun out of his belt and held it in his right hand. The sleeve of the long jacket partially covered the gun, but not entirely. Just walk in

180

and get the drop on whoever was in there. He put his left hand on the doorknob. Okay, here we go.

He pushed the door open slowly, carefully, then realized that wouldn't do. Got to move fast. Catch them by surprise.

With a hard shove and a kick, he slammed the door open. He jumped inside, saw the startled expressions on the faces of two officers, pointed the gun at them and yelled, "Reach." His voice was a little out of control.

They didn't move.

"Hands up." He wished he could fire a shot at the ceiling as a warning. Still they didn't move.

Quickly, Tim backed into a corner of the room where he could watch them and where no one could come up behind him. "I'm warning you, get your hands up."

"What in thunderation . . . ?" The officer had a round red face and a handlebar moustache. He was sitting at the desk, and the other officer, a short, fat man, was standing beside it.

Tim raised the pistol to eye level and squinted down the barrel. "All right, goddammit, I'm gonna blow a hole right between your eyes." He tried to put some menace in his voice, but it didn't come out exactly right.

"Who . . . what?" The one sitting at the desk stood slowly. "What the . . . what do you want?"

"A couple of your prisoners, that's what." Tim finally got his voice under control. "Now do you get your hands up, or do I shoot holes in both of you?"

They raised their hands.

"Now. Get away from that desk. Get over there by

that jail door." He shouted the next order, "Move your asses."

They followed his instructions.

"Turn around."

"Look here, mister, you're in a lot of trouble. You're committing a serious crime. You can't threaten an officer of the law."

"Do it, goddammit."

They turned their backs to him.

Keeping his gun on them, Tim stepped up behind them, and one at a time, took their pistols from the holsters and placed them on the desk. The guns were nickle-plated double-action six shooters. Probably .38 caliber. Tim considered using one of their guns in place of the worthless heavier pistol, but decided against it. He didn't want to shoot anyone.

"Now open that door."

"Can't. Ain't got the key."

"You're lying. The keys are in the desk. Get them and move slow. One wrong move and you're a dead cop."

They didn't move.

"You." Tim prodded the short, fat one in the back with the barrel of the Navy Colt. "Open that desk and take the keys out. And make sure you take nothing but the keys."

"Now look here, mister."

Tim put the gun at the back of the man's head, prodded him with it. "One little twitch of the finger and your head will be splattered all over that door."

That did it. "D—don't. I'll get the keys."

"Get 'em."

The short, fat one was scared now. He moved with slow careful steps to the desk, opened the drawer, and took out the ring of keys.

"Unlock the door."

When the steel door opened on creaking hinges, Tim herded the two officers down the corridor ahead of him. Prisoners saw what was happening and came to their cell doors and stared with open mouths.

"Straight ahead," Tim ordered. .

"Mister," a prisoner said, "get me out, too. Get me out, will you?"

"Turn left. Stop here."

She was sitting on her bunk, head down.

"El—" He caught himself. "Miss Burford. Come here."

She gasped when she looked up. "What? Who?" And then she recognized the bandana and his eyes. She knew who he was.

"Hurry up."

"Don't do this, uh, John. Don't get yourself in trouble."

"Get up and get over here." To the short, fat officer, he said, "Open the door. Do it, goddammit."

Still moving carefully, the officer inserted the key, turned it. The door opened a crack. The girl stood and walked uncertainly to the door. A tin plate and a tin fork lay on the floor behind her, and a toilet bucket sat in the far corner.

"Come on, hurry."

Her steps quickened and she was through the door. She stood there with a question on her face, stood there in the shapeless gray jail dress.

"Where's J—Mr. Burford?"

"I think he's around the corner."

"Let's go." Tim prodded the short, fat officer in the

side with the gun barrel. "You know where he is."

The officer led the way around the corner of a row of cells and stopped before a cell that held a half-dozen steel bunks and men. One of the men recognized the girl and came to the door. He had a hook on the end of his left arm.

"Open it," Tim barked.

The key was inserted and the door swung open.

"Out. All of you."

Men poured out of the cell and two of them started running down the corridor. "Stop," Tim yelled. "Stop or I'll shoot." They stopped. "Get back here." They came back, eyes on the gun in Tim's hand.

"All right. We're leaving first, then the rest of you can go. You," he barked at the officers, "get inside."

The two stepped gingerly into the cell. Tim took the keys, slammed the cell door and locked it. "All right, Burford, both of you, walk ahead of me. Walk, don't run. The rest of you, stay behind me."

Without saying a word, the girl and the man with the hook on his arm walked down the corridor to the door, stopped. The other prisoners followed, but stayed a good distance behind.

"Wait a second," Tim said, "I'll take a look." Standing beside the door, he peered into the outer room. It was empty. But not for long.

A tall officer in full uniform came in from outside, saw the cell door open, saw the outer office was empty, and grabbed for the pistol on his right hip.

"Reach." It ws the only thing Tim could think of to say as he stepped into the room. When the officer found himself looking up the bore of a big pistol in the hand of a masked man, his hands dropped to his side.

"Over here," Tim shouted. "One wrong move and you're dead."

The officer did as ordered, moving stiffly. "In here." Tim motioned him through the door. "Get his gun."

Quickly, the man with the hook on his left wrist pulled the gun from its holster with his right hand. He started to cock the hammer back, then realized it didn't need to be cocked.

"March." To the man and girl, Tim said, "Wait here."

They waited while Tim marched the officer to the cell and locked him inside with his fellow officers.

Running now, afraid more police would show up, Tim got back to the outer office, tucked the big pistol inside his belt, and said, "Let's get outside. Fast."

He led the way, stopped in the door, and looked around, then ran for a dark alley a hundred feet ahead. The man and girl followed him, their boots clomping on the hard-packed dirt. In the alley, in the dark, he stopped.

The five other prisoners ran outside and scattered in all directions.

"Joe." Tim was breathing hard, not so much from the short run as from the tension. "I hope you know where to go and hide, because I sure as hell don't."

"Tim? Tim Higgins?"

"Yeah." Tim pulled the bandana off his face.

"What're you doin' this for?"

"Never mind. Do you know a place to hide?"

"Yeah, I know a place."

"Well then," Tim said, trying to bring his breathing under control, "let's haul our freight out of here."

Chapter Twenty-one

Now it was Joseph Holt who led the way. Down an alley, across a street, down another alley. They ran, their boots making too much noise and attracting the attention of barking dogs. In a dark alley south of downtown, behind a factory of some kind, they stopped, gasping for breath.

"Got to find an alley that goes east," Joseph Holt wheezed. "I wish there wasn't so many dogs."

"How . . . how far are we going?" Tim asked.

" 'Bout another mile. We've got horses there."

They stood a moment, giving their lungs a chance to recover, then went on, walking fast. The girl had to run at times to keep up with them. At Broadway, they picked an intersection that wasn't lighted. "Best walk natural," Joseph Holt said, "till we get across the street."

Trying to look like three people out for an evening stroll, they walked across Broadway, then ran up a dark street. "The damn alleys all go the wrong way," Joseph Holt panted. "Have to stay in the street."

"Run for the shadows," Tim said.

Twice they stopped in the shadows of houses while horse-drawn carriages went past. The carriages carried lamps. Dogs barked, but no one paid any attention to the dogs.

"Not much farther. You doin' all right, Ellen?"

"Yeah. Don't worry about me."

They went on, alternating between running and walking. Finally, about the time Tim thought he couldn't run anymore, Joseph Holt turned down another alley. He stopped behind a barn.

"Here. Here's where we left our horses."

"Why here?"

"One of the bunch lives here. Come on, let's get inside."

A barn door opened on rusty hinges, and Joseph Holt said, "Get in and I'll shut the door." They groped their way in. The door was closed. Tim could smell horses and hear them as they blew their noses and shuffled their feet. Joseph Holt struck a match. He held it until it burned his fingers, then dropped it and stepped on it.

"That horse there is your good bay horse, Tim. I traded for him." He struck another match. "Over here is your good saddle. That brown horse over there is Ellen's."

"How . . . ?" Tim started to ask about his bay horse, but Joseph Holt cut him off.

"Let's be quiet a minute and see if anybody followed us."

They listened, trying to control their breathing. But Tim had to whisper, "Who lives in the house?"

It was the girl who answered, also whispering, "One

of the gang. We have to be quiet."

"Why . . . ?" Tim shut up, realizing the girl was serious about being quiet.

They listened. All they heard was the horses, chewing hay, blowing their noses, and moving their feet. After several minutes, Joseph Holt said, "We've got to git out of here, out of town."

"I have to get some clothes," the girl said. "I can't go far in this outfit. You're lucky they didn't take your clothes, Joe."

"Yeah. Let's wait a little bit and see if there's anybody at home."

Tim heard him move, saw a dark blob at the barn door.

"I can see the house from here," Joseph Holt said. "There's no lights. Maybe I can sneak in there."

"Any clothes will do," the girl said. "Anything but this jail dress."

"All right, I know my way around in that house. I'll go see what I can find."

"Wait a minute," Tim said. "I want some answers from you two."

There was a pause before the girl spoke. "I'll tell you everything I know, Timothy, but there's a lot I don't know. Joe doesn't know all about everything, either."

Joseph Holt said, "We're thieves, Tim. I am. Ellen only came along because I asked her to. She's as honest as the day is long."

"I'm a grown woman. I knew what I was doing."

"What happened to the HL cattle?"

"They were sold."

"I know that. Who is Benjamin Jones?"

"How'd you know about him?"

188

"I asked a lot of questions. I know how the cattle got to the Denver stockyards, too."

The girl's voice was sarcastic. "I wish we had known him better."

"He took the money," Joseph Holt said. "He was supposed to meet us here and give us our share. He didn't show."

"That's why we got ourselves in jail, Timothy. Joe found Ben Jones in a bar, invited him outside and relieved him of some of his money. At gunpoint."

"Yeah, but he didn't have much with him. And now the police have got what he did have."

"I can guess the rest. You robbed him, and went back to your hotel. He and one of his pals followed you and started shooting."

"Yeah. I think we shot up ever'thing but one another."

"Uh-huh. Who lives in this house?"

"A man named Wight. Dave Wight. He was skinned out of his share, too."

Tim groped his way to the door and peered through a crack. "If he was here, there ought to be a light."

"Yeah. I'll sneak in and see what I can find. Then we've got to git out of town. I don't know how, but we've got to git."

"Yes," the girl whispered. "But we have only one horse. We can't take Tim's horse."

"No, that's your horse, Tim."

"How did he happen to be here?"

"I traded for him. Jones took both your horses after you was shot. He thought you was dead."

"Uh-huh. So he sold my gray horse at Black Hawk. You all brought a hundred and three head of stolen cattle to Denver and sold them on the market just like honest cowmen."

"That's the way of it, Tim."

"How the hell did you do that? I mean, the brand inspectors've got a book that lists all the cattle brands in the state and who they're registered to. How did Benjamin Jones get his name opposite the HL brand?"

"He knows the right people."

"What people?"

"He wouldn't say. Said just to trust him."

"And that," the girl whispered, "was our big mistake. Trusting Ben Jones."

"No-o-o." Joseph Holt's voice was loaded with sorrow. "Our biggest mistake was stealin' cattle."

"If it makes any difference to you, Tim," the girl whispered, "we won't do it again. This was my first and last time."

Tim let that sink in, then said, "Let's go see what's in the house."

"Best, I go alone."

"Huh-uh. I want to see whatever there is to see in there. I might even find some of the money the HL cattle sold for."

"All right. But you won't find any money in there. Dave's as broke as I am. And we can't be sure nobody's at home, and if they ain't they could come back any minute."

"You still got that cop's gun?"

"Yeah. You want it? I'd hate to get caught with it on me."

"All right, I'll take it. This old hogleg I've got ain't loaded, anyhow."

"I'm going in, too," the girl said.

190

"Why? You're better off here."

"No I'm not. If I can't get some clothes, I might as well go back to jail and give myself up. I wouldn't get two blocks in this getup in the daylight."

Whispering, Joseph Holt said, "Maybe you're right, but let's saddle these horses, and if anything goes wrong, I want you two to get on horseback and light out."

"We'll decide on that later," Tim said.

Groping in the dark, they saddled the horses. Tim's good bay horse was nervous, wanting out of the confinement of the barn. Then Joseph Holt opened the barn door and whispered:

"I've been in that house and I know my way around. You two follow me."

A neighbor's dog barked at them as they crept toward the back of the house. They hit the ground facedown when the neighbor's back door opened and a man looked out. Only when the man satisfied his curiosity and went back inside did they stand and make their way to the house.

At the back door, they waited while Joseph Holt tried the latch. It was hooked. "Got a pocket knife, Tim? They took mine at the jail."

"Yeah, here." Tim handed him the skinning knife from his belt holster. He heard a scraping noise and some measured breathing.

"It's open. Just took a blade between the door and the jamb. You two wait here till I make sure there's nobody at home." He handed the knife back to Tim.

They waited. Joseph Holt made very little noise as he crept into the house. Breathing with shallow breaths, they waited. A light flared inside. A match. It moved from one room to another, went out. Another light flared.

The girl whispered, "If we get away, Tim, we'll always be in your debt."

"Naw. This makes us even."

"If we had any of the proceeds from our crime, we'd give it to you."

A light was moving again, coming toward the back of the house. It went out and another match was struck. Joseph Holt whispered, "They ain't here. Let's git it and git out. Foller me."

Striking matches, Joseph Holt led the way through a kitchen into a living room and then into a bedroom. The room held little furniture, only a bed on a wooden frame and two empty fruit crates full of soiled clothes. The girl went through the clothes.

"I know there's no money here, Tim," Joseph Holt whispered. "Old Wight got snookered out of his share, too. But I'll look around." He left the room, and Tim heard him go back to the kitchen.

He also heard the rustling of some clothes, and he reached into his own shirt pocket for a match, struck it.

"Don't," the girl whispered, and Tim saw why.

She was standing in her briefs, about to put her foot into the leg of a pair of men's pants. For a second, Tim stared at her, fascinated. Maybe two or three seconds. He'd almost forgotten she was a girl. Now there was no doubt. Slim, but curved in all the right places. Little Ellen Olsen had grown up.

"Timothy," she pleaded.

"Oh, uh, excuse me." He shook out the match.

Footsteps. Hurrying. Joseph Holt was back. "Somebody's comin'. I heard 'em on the front porch."

He was right. The front door opened, and heavy boots clomped across the living room floor. The three in the bedroom stood perfectly still, trying not to breathe. A lamp was lit.

Men's voices. "Who in hell coulda busted them two out of the hoosegow?"

"You sure it was them two?"

"Goddamn right, I'm sure. It's all over town by now. Gave the name of Burford, but you know goddamn well it's them two."

"They'll be comin' here. They think you beat me out of my share, too, and their hosses're out in the barn."

"Better go look. I wonder if they've got a gun."

"Whoever busted 'em out has, and that Joe Holt is dangerous in the dark even without a gun. That hook on his arm could rip a man's throat out before he knows it."

"Well, we got to go take a look. Got another lamp?"

"Yeah. It's in the bedroom."

Tim heard Ellen's sudden intake of breath. He heard Joseph Holt whisper. "Get that gun handy. One of 'em is Ben Jones."

Chapter Twenty-two

He was coming. Tim gripped the police officer's gun and thumbed the hammer back. That was a mistake. The racheting sound of a gun being cocked was easy to recognize. And the gun was double-action and didn't have to be cocked, anyway.

"Hey," a man shouted. "Somebody's in there. They're in there."

"Shit. Gawdamighty damn."

Joseph Holt stood beside Tim and whispered, "If you don't want to shoot somebody, give me the gun."

"No, I'll do it."

They were quiet in the living room. The lamp was blown out, leaving the house dark.

"They'll be comin'," Joseph Holt whispered. "They're gonna come in fast and throw lead in all directions. Best git down on the floor."

Again he was right.

They hit the floor when they heard footsteps coming toward them. A gun blazed. Two guns. The room was filled with gunfire. The whole world seemed to explode with gunfire.

Joseph Holt yelled, "Shoot, Tim." His voice was drowned out by two more rapid shots.

Both guns were big caliber. Fire shot out of the barrels. Tim aimed at a gunflash and squeezed the trigger. The .38 had little recoil, and its bark was puny compared to the .45s'. He fired again, then rolled over once to make himself a moving target. A .45 boomed, and a heavy slug dug a splintery furrow in the floor where Tim had been.

Taking aim from his position on the floor, Tim squeezed the trigger again. The .38 popped. A man yelled, "Shit, I'm hit."

Another gunflash came from the doorway, and Tim fired.

A body hit the floor.

Silence. Except for heavy breathing. No one moved. Tim wanted to move, to strike a match, see what had happened. That would be foolish. A man holding a light would be a perfect target. He stayed on the floor, on his belly.

Someone over near the door started groaning. But no one moved. For several long moments, the only sound was the groaning. And breathing. And the neighbor's dog barking outside.

Who was hit? And how many? Was Ellen or Joe Holt hit? Tim wanted to find out. He had to find out. But not yet. Wait. If he made a sound or moved he would attract more shots from a .45. Stay still.

How long could a man wait? Or a woman? Something had to happen. Someone had to do something. Tim could hear breathing on his left, and he guessed it was the girl. No sound came from Joe Holt's end of the room. Whoever was over there by the door could hear the girl breathing and he would fire a shot in her direction. If she wasn't already shot she would be. Unless he did something. Got to do something.

How many shots left in his gun? Hell, he didn't know. No more than a couple. All right, waste one, but only one.

No use taking aim. Can't see anybody to shoot at, anyway. Shoot and move. Tim fired in the direction of the doorway and immediately rolled to his right, away from the girl. A .45 boomed. Tim heard the slug tear into the floor.

Then quiet again. Except for the groaning. The groaning changed to a raspy kind of breathing. No one moved. Gradually, the breathing slowed and stopped.

Now there was movement over by the door. Then a voice said, "Ben?"

The voice came from the other side of the doorway, from the living room. There was no answer.

"Ben?"

Still no answer.

Bootsteps. Moving fast. The front door opened. Boots clomped across the porch. Quiet.

"Tim?" Joseph Holt's voice came from his left. "I think they're gone."

"Yeah. Ellen? You there?"

"Yes. I'm all right."

"I'm gonna strike a match, Tim. Don't shoot."

A match flared. It moved, stopped over a prone figure. Went out. Tim struck a match, moved over to the girl. She was getting up from the floor, wearing a man's wool pants turned up at the bottom. A tight belt held them up.

Another match was struck. "It's Ben Jones. I think he's dead."

For a while they stood there in the dark, not knowing what to do or say next. Then Joseph Holt struck another match. "We got to git," he said. "All that racket's gonna bring somebody. Somebody's prob'ly gone for the police already."

"Yeah. Ellen, you ready to go?"

"Yes. I managed to change clothes before they . . ."

"Git out to the horses, you two."

"What are you gonna do, Joe?"

"I don't know. Run, I reckon. But I want you two horseback and gone."

"We'll all go. Ellen's horse will carry double."

"Go where?"

"To the alley behind my aunt's house. She lives on Pearl Street. I've got my gray horse there."

"Then what?"

A terrible urgency came over Tim. "Let's get out of this house and then decide."

"Right. Just a minute." Joseph Holt struck another match and bent over the downed man. "This sonofabitch cheated us out of our money. And did you hear what they said? Dave Wight was in on the scheme, too. He only pretended he was cheated." The light went out, and Joseph Holt grunted with the exertion of turning the man over. "Yep. He's got some on 'im. Now let's git."

They ran out the back door and headed toward the barn. The dog in the next yard barked and snarled. The neighbor's back door opened and a man stood in it, holding a rifle.

"Hey. What's goin' on over there?"

They were inside the barn, groping for the horses. "Whoa, Brownie," the girl said. "Whoa, now."

Tim dropped the police officer's gun in one of the hay mangers, but made certain the old Army Colt was still held in place by his belt.

She was the first outside, leading her horse by the bridle reins, and was the first mounted. Joseph Holt followed, leading Tim's bay horse. "Come on, Tim," the girl said. "Here, take my hand."

She had her left foot out of the stirrup and was holding her right hand behind her back. Tim took her hand, put his foot in the stirrup and swung up behind the saddle. The horse jumped once, and the girl slacked up on the reins and let it run. Joseph Holt was mounted too now, and the two horses galloped down the alley, hooves pounding the hard-packed dirt.

"Go west," Tim said, and the girl reined the horse to the left. "A couple of blocks, then north."

At the entrance to the alley behind Aunt Josephine's house, Tim said, "Slow up. Try not to attract any attention." The horses slowed to a walk. "Here. Right here." Tim was whispering again. He slid off the horse.

Joseph Holt got down beside him, barely visible in the dark. "Here, Tim. I took this roll off Ben Jones's body. It's yours. He—we—stole it from you. Stole your cattle, I mean. I don't know how much's there."

The girl whispered, "What's next, Tim?"

"You're the boss, Tim," Joseph Holt said.

"Here's what you two are gonna do." Tim realized he was talking like a ranch cow boss, but he knew it was up to him to make decisions now. "You're gonna get out of town tonight and head back to Shiprock. You're gonna take my bay horse there and my gray horse and some of this money, and you're gonna stop somewhere tomorrow and buy some chuck and blankets, and you're going home."

"What are you going to do, Tim?" He could feel her presence, and he liked the feeling.

"I've got things to do here." He took a rubber band off the roll of money Joseph Holt had handed him and peeled off several bills. "I don't know how much this is, but take it. You'll need it."

"That's your money, Tim."

"Take it. Now listen, I'm loaning you my horses, and I want those horses taken to the HL. Tell John I'm staying in Denver a while and coming home on a train. Tell him I loaned you the horses. And, listen here, I want those horses taken home in good shape. You run them too hard and I'll come looking for you when I get back. This gray horse carried me up and down a lot of mountains. Take good care of him. Got it?"

Instead of waiting for an answer, he went into his aunt's stable, saddled the gray horse, and led him out. "Take good care of him."

"Shore will, Tim. But you know I can't show my face at the HL."

"I'll take them back," the girl said. "And they'll be well cared for."

"All right. Now get horseback and get going."

"Tim, I . . ." Joseph Holt's voice stumbled. "I don't know why you did this, but . . . well . . ."

"You used to be a good man, Joe. I'm betting on you."

"Tim?" Her voice was soft, all female. "Will we see

199

you again?"

"Yeah. I've got some things to do here, and then I'll go back to the HL."

The horses left on a high trot. Her voice came to him as they disappeared in the dark, "Good-bye, Tim."

He stood looking in the direction they had gone, wishing he could have gone with them, feeling terribly alone again. "Lord," he whispered to himself, "I wish to hell this whole mess was over."

It was the back door opening that brought him out of his black mood. "Timothy? Is that you?"

"Yes, Aunt Josie. I'll be in in a minute." Quickly, he changed clothes in the dark stable and hid his uncle's clothes and the gun under a pile of hay. He'd come back tomorrow, retrieve them and put them back in the house where he'd found them. As soon as his aunt went on her daily walk to the grocery store.

Having to lie to his aunt made his mood even blacker. He hated to lie to her. He wouldn't cause her any trouble for anything in the world.

"It's awfully late, Timothy."

"I ran into a man I know and I sold him my gray horse. That's what we were doing out back."

"Someone you know?"

"Yeah. From the year I worked at Daniels and Fisher." Lord, forgive me, he thought.

"Well, how did you get along with that girl, that Mary Jane McCeogh?"

"Just fine. We played cards. I was walking home when I met my friend."

"Well, I'm going back to bed, Timothy. Goodnight."

"Goodnight, Aunt Josie." Dear Aunt Josie, if you only knew. You wouldn't believe it. A couple of weeks ago I wouldn't have believed it myself. Forgive me, Aunt Josie.

In bed, he couldn't sleep. He couldn't get it out of his mind. Everything that had happened. His horses. They wouldn't be hurt. Joe Holt was good to horses. One of the reasons he was a cowboy was his love for horses. Ellen wouldn't hurt anything. Not little Ellen Olsen, the kid who could never keep her stockings up. The horses would be fine, but there was something else on his mind. Something he couldn't shut out.

Lying in the dark, he squinched his eyes tight, trying but it wouldn't go away.

He'd killed a man.

Chapter Twenty-three

The wad of money he'd stuffed in his pants pocket was forgotten until he put his pants on the next morning. In the privacy of his room he counted it. Four hundred dollars, all in fifty-dollar bills. If the whole roll had consisted of fifties, then he'd given Joseph Holt a hundred and fifty dollars. Maybe two hundred. That ought to be enough to buy them all the chuck and blankets they needed to get back home in comfort. But it wasn't anywhere near what a hundred and three head of prime beeves would bring on the market.

Someone owed the HL a lot more money.

At breakfast he told his aunt, "Now that I've sold my horse, I've got enough money to buy some clothes. I could sure use some."

"Buy some nice clothes, Timothy, so you'll look nice when you see that girl again."

Passing up the six-story mercantile on Sixteenth Street, Tim went back to the stockman's store on Larimer. "Hey there, young feller, how's the head?" The proprietor was all smiles.

"Healing fast. Got some boots that'll fit me?"

"Got all sizes, colors, and styles. Expect you're interested in riding boots."

He bought some new calfskin boots, a shirt, some socks and underclothes, and tried on a pair of new denim pants. "Naw. You have to wash this kind at least three times before they fit right. What else have you got?"

"Gabardines. That's what you need. Look at these."

The pants had a crease down the front, and they looked good with the new boots. When he left the store, he carried his old clothes in a paper bag, and when he boarded a streetcar he could feel the eyes of other passengers on him, on his new stockman's clothes. Aunt Josephine was thrilled.

"Now you look like a member of a successful ranching family ought to look."

When she took her daily stroll to the grocery store, he hurried to the stable, gathered his uncle's clothes and gun, and carefully put them back where he'd found them. He sat a while, trying to decide what to do next, and decided to walk to the capitol building and see the Secretary of State.

His boots squeaked, telling everyone they were new, and when he entered Colorado's new stone capitol building, they pounded loudly on the marble floor.

"Where," he asked a young woman hurrying by, "is the Secretary of State's office?"

She pointed to a sign at the other end of the hall, across the rotunda, and stared at him as he clomp-clomped in that direction.

Inside the office, a big room with a half-dozen men and women bent over desks, he was confronted by a

203

long counter and a sign at the end of it. The sign read: "State Employees Only. All Others Keep Out." He stood at the counter.

"Yes?" It was another young woman, all business in her long blue dress with white cuffs and a collar.

"I'd like to see the Secretary of State, if you please, ma'am."

"He's busy. What do you want?"

"I'd like to check on a cattle brand."

"Which brand? I'll look it up."

"It's the HL."

"The HL?" She went to a series of metal filing cabinets on the other side of the room, ran her fingers down one, then halfway down another. Squatting, she took a close look at the lettering on the drawer, pulled the drawer out. Her fingers moved swiftly over a row of manila folders, and she picked one.

"The HL, you said?" She carried the folder to the long counter and opened it. Tim tried to read it upside down, couldn't. "The HL. Hmmm. Oh, here it is. It's registered to a Benjamin Jones."

Tim's mouth dropped open. He sputtered, "But it can't be. There's a mistake."

"No, there isn't," the young woman said. "It's right here."

"Let me see it."

"I can't do that."

"Why not?"

"Mr. Rondeau doesn't allow it."

"Who is he? The Secretary of State?"

"Yes." She closed the manila folder and hugged it to her breast.

"Tell him I want to see him."

"Oh, he doesn't like to be bothered. He's very busy."

Tim felt his face getting red. Anger was coming rapidly to the surface. "Listen." His mouth was tight and the words came through his teeth. "You tell Mr. Rondeau or whatever his name is I want to see him, and I mean right now."

Fearfully, the young woman stepped back, away from the angry man at the counter. "Yes. Yessir, I'll tell him." She hurried across the room and disappeared inside an inner office.

Trying to bring his anger under control, Tim took two deep breaths and exhaled slowly. Getting mad would accomplish nothing. Calm down.

The man who came out of the inner office wore suspenders to hold up his baggy pants. He had mutton chop sideburns, heavy jowls, and thick gray hair parted in the middle. A half-smoked cigar stuck out of his mouth. He was overweight and soft-looking, obviously a man who liked to eat well.

"Now what's this all about?" His voice was not friendly.

"Well, sir," Tim ordered himself to talk with a civil tongue, "my name is Timothy Higgins. My dad, John Higgins, owns the HL Ranch in Parker County. The HL brand is registered in his name. But according to your records there and the brand book at the stockyards, the HL is registered to a Benjamin Jones. There has to be a mistake."

"You're who?"

With a sigh, Tim started over, but Mr. Rondeau cut him off. "Your name is Higgins? Son of John Higgins?"

"Yes, sir."

"Well, now. Let's see here." Mr. Rondeau shifted the

cigar from one side of his mouth to the other, took the folder from the young woman, and started to open it. He said, "You have other work to do, Wanda." The young woman left. "Now then." He studied the papers in the folder, shuffled them, looked up at Tim.

"It's right here. John Higgins. The HL."

"Well, then . . ." Now Tim was confused. "How did that young lady and a brand inspector at the stockyards make a mistake?"

The Secretary of State was suddenly all smiles. A good fellow. "Oh, you know how it is, you can't get good help these days. You prob'ly have the same trouble on the ranch. Mistakes are made. Look here." He took a sheet of paper from the folder and handed it to Tim. "It's as plain as day."

It was. No mistake about it. The brands were listed in alphabetical order, and opposite the HL was the name of John Higgins.

"Well, uh, could it be filed two ways? With John Higgins's name first and then the brand?"

"You betcha. We keep it all cross-filed. Wait a second." He went to the filing cabinets, ran his eyes down the one on his left, pulled open a drawer, and took out another manila folder.

"Yep," he said when he returned to the counter. "Here it is. See for yourself."

Tim looked where he pointed. John Higgins. Parker County. Brand, HL.

Puzzled, Tim shook his head. "A hundred and three head of cattle carrying the HL brand were sold at the Union Stockyards within the last week, and a brand inspector there said the brand was registered to Benjamin Jones."

206

Mr. Rondeau shook his head, too. "Can't be. They made a mistake. I'll have to check into this."

"Those cattle were stolen. How do I get paid?"

With another negative shake of his head, Mr. Rondeau said, "I don't have anything to do with that. I just keep track of the brands. Among a thousand other things. And without enough help. We've got so much paperwork to do here our left hands don't know what our right hands are doing. And when I ask the General Assembly for a bigger budget so I can hire more help, they squawk and say the taxpayers won't stand for it. I can only do so much with the budget I have to work with. Now, is there anything else I can do for you, young fella?"

Tim tried to think of something else to say. He could think of nothing. He stammered, "N-no. I guess not."

Walking back to Aunt Josephine's house, Tim ran it all through his mind again and again. Somebody had made a bad mistake. Or somebody was pulling something crooked. Somehow a cattle thief named Benjamin Jones had got the papers switched so it looked like the HL brand belonged to him. Now, the thing to do was to find out exactly where the switch happened. And who switched them. Where to start?

"That's easy," he mumbled to himself. "At the Union Stockyards, and that brand book the brand inspectors use. Only maybe that won't be so easy."

He changed back to his working clothes, and his old boots felt better on his feet. Thinking back, he wished he'd kept his gray horse. The streetcars didn't go near the stockyards, and he needed transportation. But he couldn't have known he'd have to go back to the stockyards.

A streetcar stopped for him on East Colfax, and he changed cars once to get as far to the north and east as the public transportation system went. Then he walked. His stomach reminded him he hadn't had any lunch. Hell with lunch.

By the time he got to the administration building it was late afternoon, and the brand inspectors' office was closed and locked. All right, one of them had to be out in the yards somewhere. Walk some more.

Down stockyard alleys he walked, past pens of cattle and sheep. He made his way to the other side of the tracks, to the packing house section, and there he found the brand inspector named Garrison. No use talking to him. He wouldn't tell a feller the way out of a burning building. Where's the other one, the fat one?

He found Theodore Wilkins clipping the hair away from a brand on a steer that was held motionless in a squeeze chute. The hair had grown over the brand so it couldn't be read otherwise.

"Mr. Wilkins?"

The fat man grunted and looked over his shoulder. "Hello, young man."

"I'd like to talk to you when you get time."

"That's gonna be a while. I got to read the brands on about forty head here."

"Well, I'm sure sorry to bother you, sir, but I wonder if I could have another look at your brand book?"

Grunting with the exertion of reaching through the chute bars, Theodore Wilkins said, "Why d'you wanta do that?"

"There's something crazy about who the HL is

registered to."

"Okay." The fat man straightened up, put his clippers on a bench, and picked up a black, well-worn ledger. "It's alphabetical. Be careful with it."

Tim turned the pages until he came to the HL. "Well, for . . . what in hell's going on here?"

"What's the matter now?"

"Says here the HL belongs to John Higgins. That book you showed me in your office has the HL belonging to Benjamin Jones."

"Yeah." Theodore Wilkins scratched his jaw. "As I recollect, it does."

"How can that be?"

"There's a mistake somewhere."

"Whose mistake?"

"You got me there, son. It could be Walt's, or it could be . . ."

The steer was let out of the chute and another was run in. A man in bib overalls with a lump of tobacco in his cheek jerked a long handle down and a U-shaped length of pipe dropped behind the steer's head, holding him helpless.

"I got work to do, son. Catch me later and I'll try to help you."

Tim watched the man work. Some of the brands could be read by feel, but others had to have the hair clipped away. Tim remembered the first time he'd handled the irons for a branding crew. He'd picked a red-hot iron out of the fire and had been scolded by his dad.

"You don't havta burn hell out of 'em," White Shirt had said. "Just burn 'em enough to make a scar."

Tim had learned to rub the too-hot irons in the dust

209

to cool them off.

The stockyard pen at Denver was still full of cattle when he gave up and left. He'd go to the cafe behind the administration building, get a sandwich, and come back. Thinking he had plenty of time, he ate a beef sandwich and drank a cup of coffee. But when he went back, the pen was empty and Theodore Wilkins was gone.

"Shit. Goddamn. More walking."

He walked back to the administration building and found it closed. Locked. Looking at the western horizon, he saw the sun sinking out of sight.

"Dammit all to hell, anyway," he muttered, walking back to the streetcar tracks. But as he walked, he realized the man he wanted to see again wasn't Theodore Wilkins, but the Secretary of State. There was something damned funny about that manila folder. More of his dad's philosophy came to his mind:

Never trust a politician. He can pat you on the back with one hand and stick a knife in your gut with the other.

Mr. Rondeau was elected. He was a politician.

"Yeah," Tim muttered, "I want another meeting with that sonofabitch."

Chapter Twenty-four

Aunt Josephine was full of news at supper. "It's all anybody is talking about. Two people broke out of jail, and a man shot to death in a house on Jewell Street. The police think it's tied together. It's all in the paper too."

Tim put down his knife and fork, grabbed the paper, and scanned the story on page one. Police had gone to the house and found the body, identified as Benjamin Jones. Two bullet wounds, one in the left thigh and one in the center of the chest. After daylight, the police had searched the barn and found the gun taken from an officer at the city jail. They believed the fatal shots had come from that gun. They had also found evidence that two horses had been kept in the barn, and they deduced that the jailbreakers had fled on horseback. After checking criminal records, police discovered that the dead man had been in trouble with the law and had served time in the state prison at Canon City for armed robbery. The shooting, police surmised, had been the result of a falling out among thieves, and they believe

Benjamin Jones was the masked man who had forced the jailers at gunpoint to release a man and woman named Burford.

It was good news and bad news. Benjamin Jones was blamed for the jailbreak. Tim was in the clear there. But law officers were looking for a man and woman on horseback.

Worrisome thought went through Tim's mind: I hope they got plumb out of the city before the cops found that gun, and I hope they didn't stop for supplies anywhere near a telegraph station. If they got clear of Denver and stayed away from a telegraph, they'll make it. The cops have no idea where to look. How could I have been so dumb as to leave that gun in the barn?

Aunt Josephine was talking. "It's getting so a body isn't safe anymore, what with men shooting at each other in a hotel lobby, and people breaking out of jail, and men shooting at each other in a house on Jewell Street. I liked Denver better before it got so big and so full of criminals. A body isn't safe. I'm going to start locking the doors at night."

Tim was quiet until his aunt asked, "What's worrying you, Timothy? You look like a person with worries. Do you feel well?"

"Huh? Oh, yeah, I feel fine. I guess I was thinking about John's cattle and what happened to them. There's something mighty strange going on in the Secretary of State's office, Aunt Josie, and I've got to find out what it is."

"Why don't you let the police take care of that? That's what they're for."

Not wanting to talk about it, Tim shrugged and said, "Yeah, that's what I ought to do."

212

Pretending only a casual interest in the newspaper, he turned pages and scanned the headlines. Another one caught his eye and he read the story. A man identified as David Wight had been found lying on the sidewalk on East Colfax and had been taken to the general hospital. A doctor there said he was suffering from a bullet wound in the right side. Mr. Wight would make no statements to the police.

As she stacked the supper dishes, his aunt asked, "When are you going to see that girl again? That Mary Jane McCeogh."

"Oh, uh, tonight. Yeah, now that I've got some new clothes, I want her and her mother to see me dressed like something besides a wild Indian."

"I'd advise you to get a haircut, too, but with that wound on your head, maybe you'd best wait a while. By the way, how is that wound?"

"It's a lot better. It's scabbing over. It's healing."

Aunt Josephine shook her head sadly. "If you'd asked me I would have advised you to go to a doctor, but you're almost a grown man." She was silent a moment, chewing her food thoughtfully. "Anyway, I'm glad you've found a nice girl."

Mary Jane McCeogh answered his knock on the door, and instead of asking him in she stepped outside, shut the door behind her, and put her arms around his neck. Her lips were inviting, and it was an invitation he couldn't pass up.

"I hoped you'd come last night, Timothy. I've been thinking about you."

The kiss left him a little breathless, and he tried to

213

cover that by joking. "If I hang around too much you'll get tired of me."

"Huh-uh." She offered her lips again.

"Lordy," he said when she drew back. "You're gonna have me following you around like a lost puppy."

Giggling, she said, "Perhaps we'd better go in. Mother will want to know who knocked."

Inside, Mrs. McCeogh greeted him warmly, and her eyes told him she approved of his new clothes. "I'm sorry that Mr. McCeogh isn't here," she said. "He'll be back tomorrow, however, and I'm sure he'll want to see you again. Have you had dinner?"

"Yes, ma'am. I just dropped by to say hello, just to keep Mary Jane from forgetting about me."

"That's not likely," Mary Jane smiled. "I won't ever forget the handsome young rancher who saved my life."

"Will you be going back to the ranch soon, Mr. Higgins?"

"Pretty soon. I, uh, have some more business to take care of here."

The girl pouted. "Then I won't see you anymore."

"Oh, you probably will. I don't expect to stay at the ranch very long. I'll probably be back." It occurred to him he was being misleading without intending to. But dammit, he wasn't going to tell them about his family problems.

"Well, if you'll excuse me, Mr. Higgins, I'll leave you young people to visit." Mrs. McCeogh left the room.

"Would you like to go for a walk, Timothy? It's a beautiful fall evening."

Would he ever. He could still taste her lips, and he couldn't get enough of that.

They walked to East Colfax and back, talking about nothing in particular, then sat in a glider on the front porch in the dark. She scooted close, her knee touching his knee. Her kiss was warm and exciting. It made his blood boil and his loins ache. Lordy.

It was Mrs. McCeogh who brought them with a jerk out of their embrace. She opened the door and said, "I thought I heard voices out here. It's getting late, Mary Jane."

Walking back to his aunt's house, he felt a spring in his step and a joy at being alive. "Yep," he said to himself, "Tim Higgins has got a girl. I'm in love."

Then he recalled the night before, and his spirits dropped into the dirt. What would she think of him if she knew about that? He was a criminal, not fit to be courting a beautiful, gentle girl like Mary Jane. He had killed a man.

Thinking of that reminded him of the business he had to take care of. He hadn't come to Denver to socialize. What to do? Go see the Secretary of State again? What would that accomplish? He'd say the same thing he'd said this morning. An honest mistake. Incompetent help.

Honest mistake, hell. A mistake that costs somebody thousands of dollars can't be kissed off simply by calling it an honest mistake. There wasn't anything honest about it.

So, what to do?

He reached a decision, and his steps quickened. He wished he were wearing his old boots and faded denim pants, but he couldn't go back to his aunt's house and change. He'd have to do some explaining, and he'd have to lie again.

Instead of going back to Colfax he turned down a less traveled east-west street and stayed in the shadows as much as possible. Oak trees had been planted along the streets in that part of the city, and they promised to provide beauty and shade in the future. He stayed close to them, wishing his new boots weren't so noisy.

It was a short walk to the rear of the state capitol, and he hugged the wall, looking for an entrance. A door on the south side ground level was locked, of course. The front entrance was too easy to see from the street, and it was no doubt locked, too. There was no way in, except to break in.

He went to the rear of the building again, still hugging the wall and trying to make himself invisible every time a carriage went by. The electric street light on Colfax illuminated the north side of the building. He stayed on the south side. Finally, he found what he was looking for. A window.

It was shoulder high and big enough for a bear to crawl through. But it, too, was locked. No doubt everything was locked. Only one thing to do. It was a crazy thing to do, but he was getting used to doing crazy things.

Balancing himself on one foot, he pulled off his right boot, took a couple of practice swings to get the feel of it, then swung the heel against the windowpane. Glass shattered. He swung again and broke out more glass. Then he squatted under the window, pulled his boot on, and waited, eyes and ears tense.

For a long while, he waited. Nothing. Nobody.

Carefully, he stood, felt for the windowsill. A sharp piece of broken glass stung his hand. Damn. He took off the boot again and broke out all the glass in the lower half of the window, stopped, listened.

Either do it or give up and get the hell out of here.

He pulled himself up and got his chest across the windowsill. Then his stomach. His belt snagged on the windowsill. He squirmed, got it free. Hanging upside down inside the window now, he reached for the floor. Where the hell is the floor? His thighs were on the windowsill, slipping. Then he fell inside. He hit the floor with a thump that could have been heard throughout the building. Jaysus H. Christmas. Hide. Find something to get behind. Darker than a stack of black cats. He got up and collided with a desk. Hands in front of him, he groped his way through the room and into the corridor. Still groping, he found another office door. He ducked inside and stood still, back against a wall. If men came to check out the noise they'd go to the room with the broken window. Stay here. Listen.

He listened and shook his head in disbelief. No one was guarding the building. No one awake, anyhow. Now. Find the Secretary of State's office. Let's see, it was on the second floor, on the south side of the rotunda. Remembering that the ground outside sloped down from the rear of the building to the front, he believed he was on the second floor. The rotunda ought to be easy to find.

Swearing under his breath at the squeaky new boots, he crept down the corridor. His left hand against the wall was his guide. Damn boots. Was that a light ahead? A dim one. Seems to be coming from the floor.

Uh-oh. The rotunda. The light was down in the rotunda. On the ground floor. He wasn't alone in the building.

217

Or was he? Maybe somebody had left a lamp burning. Or were there electric lights in the state capitol? He couldn't remember. Got to look down there. Easy. Damn boots.

He made his way to the rotunda and the railing around it, looked down. The light was brighter down there. A guard? If there was a guard, he was deaf. Or asleep. A friend or a relative of somebody important. Like to know if there's anybody down there, but damned if I'm going down there and look. Move on. Quiet.

Though he'd never picked up the smoking habit, Tim had the outdoorsmen's practice of always carrying matches. When he thought he was in front of the Secretary of State's office, he struck one, held it up. Nope. Move on. Damn boots.

Now his left hand told him he was in front of another office, one with a frosted glass pane in the door. Another match proved it to be the office he was looking for. He turned the knob.

Shit. Goddamn. Hell.

It was locked.

Tim felt the hope drain out of him, leaving him empty, weak. What the hell was he going to do now? He couldn't break the glass. The noise would echo up and down the corridor and wake up a dead man. Give up, his mind told him. This was a damn fool thing to do anyway. Get out. Go back to Aunt Josie's. Turn this whole mess over to the police.

The police? What would they do?

Got to get in there.

He remembered how easily Joseph Holt had opened the back door of the house on Jewell Street. Just slipped a knife blade between the door and the door jamb. The flare from another match showed him what kind of lock it was: a new one, brass, with a small keyhole. Okay, try the knife.

The skinning knife he'd carried on his belt was in his bedroom with his old clothes, but he had a small folding knife in his pants pocket. He opened the blade and poked it between the door and the jamb, right where the lock was. He pushed it to the handle, pulled it out, pushed it in again. He felt resistance. He pushed. Something gave. Hold it there. Now try the knob. The knob turned. The door cracked open.

He realized he'd been holding his breath, and he exhaled audibly. Quiet, dammit. Listen. Get inside. If anybody came to investigate he'd be too easy to spot in the corridor.

Quickly, he stepped inside and closed the door.

Chapter Twenty-five

Darker than the inside of a hip pocket. He listened for possible footsteps in the corridor, then struck another match. The glass pane in the door was frosted, but a light would show through it, anyway. Couldn't do a damn thing without a light. He went around the long counter to the filing cabinets on the far side of the room. His match burned his fingers and he dropped it.

Only one way to do it: pull one of the little brass chains that hung from the ceiling and turn on one of the electric lights. First, he went back to the door and made certain it was locked. The lock, he'd already noticed, was a new one, and if he was lucky, the watchman, if there was one, wouldn't have a key for it. That brought a smug smile to Tim's lips. The Secretary of State didn't want anyone, not even a watchman, looking in his office.

The lightswitch chain nearest the filing cabinets was over his head, and by waving his arms he found it and pulled. A naked light bulb in the ceiling came on, illuminating that part of the room. Again, Tim listened for footsteps. His eyes studied the small cards on the ends of each filing cabinet drawer until he found one that read "G to L." Opening it, he took out the H folder.

The brands were there, alphabetically, with a page for each brand. There was an H Cross, and HB Bar and an HL. The name on the HL page was John Higgins, Parker County. Strange. Damned strange.

He turned to another bank of cabinets and ran his eyes down the drawers until he came to another marked G to L. He found the H file, opened it. Higgins, John, a drawing of a steer and the HL. Aw, for crying out loud. Hmm. Just out of curiosity, he took out the J file.

Uh-huh. Jones, Benjamin, Gilpin County, HL.

Placing the two manila folders on top of a cabinet, he stood there a moment, puzzled. Then he opened the J file again. There was a Jones, Benjamin on another page, and opposite that the JB Bar. Tim turned more pages. They were loose, removable. Another listed Jones, Benjamin as owner of the T Cross, and still another had him owning the Mill Iron brand.

Tim got the picture then. It was as clear as springwater. Benjamin Jones was a professional thief and had managed to get several cattle brands belonging to honest ranchers registered in his name, too. He could steal cattle and prove by these papers that they were his.

But he couldn't have managed that alone. Somebody in the state government was in cahoots. And it had to be somebody in the Secretary of State's office. A clerk? Not likely.

Pulling the chain, Tim put out the light, then groped his way to the door of the inner office. Locked. Wouldn't you know it. He tried his knife blade, pushed, pulled it out, pushed again. Wouldn't work. A different kind of lock. Dammit. Frustration brought a long sigh out of him. The frustration turned to anger, and he rammed the door with his right shoulder. Rammed it again. Listened for footsteps and rammed it again. The door jamb splintered and the door opened.

Moving hastily now, Tim pulled another light string and went through the big oak desk. He found nothing of interest. A big leather-covered chair was opposite the desk, and behind that was another filing cabinet. He opened the drawer marked G to L. Found no page listing John Higgins. The J file contained no mention of Benjamin Jones.

Now what the hell?

He knew he couldn't stay in that office all night. The office window was on the front of the building, facing busy Lincoln Street. Somebody would see the light through the window and get suspicious. If there was a watchman in the building, he would wake up sooner or later. And if he was a political appointee he'd like nothing better than to catch a thief in the act. That would give him something to brag about, make everyone think he was a wide-awake guard.

With busy fingers and straining eyes, Tim looked through every file in the top drawer, then moved down to the drawer marked B. Uh-oh.

Benjamin, Hiram, the HL. Next page, Benjamin, Hiram, the JB Bar. More pages had the same man as owner of the T Cross and Mill Iron. The Secretary of State had his private files, and in case some clerk happened to go through them, he had his own peculiar way of keeping files. Hiram Benjamin and Benjamin Jones had to be the same man.

Time to go. Tim put out the light, found the files he'd

222

left in the outer office, and found the outer office door. With the three manila folders in his hand, he listened, turned the small knob on the new lock, and opened the door. The corridor was dark, but he knew the way.

Damn boots.

As he went around the rotunda he saw the light below move. Fascinated, he looked down at it. The light came into view below him. A lantern held by a bearded, barrel-bellied man in overalls. The man had a pistol in a holster on his right hip. He started up the stairs.

Now it was really time to go.

But he had to be quiet. The watchman had awakened from his nap.

Balancing himself on one foot at a time, Tim took off his new boots and carried them in one hand and the manila folders in the other as he hurried in his sock feet to the office with the broken window. Just before he ducked into the office, he looked back.

The watchman was at the top of the stairs.

Tim bumped into a desk, then a chair as he made his way to the window. Footsteps were coming. The watchman had heard.

Knowing it was useless to be quiet now, Tim pulled on his boots and went out the window headfirst.

He landed on his hands outside and dropped the manila folders. In a desperate hurry, he gathered them in the dark, then ran for the blackest spot he could find. He hit the ground under a tall tree and looked back. A lantern appeared at the window, and a bearded man's face.

"Hey," the man yelled. "Hey. Stop. Thief."

Glancing around, Tim was relieved to see no one in sight. The yells had attracted no attention. But the watchman was still yelling at the top of his voice.

"Stop. Thief."

Now it was really really time to go.

He ran until he got around a corner, then slowed to a walk, not wanting to attract attention. As he walked, his mind went over the night's events. He had proved something, but to whom? If he went to the police or the sheriff and told them what he'd found, the Secretary of State would deny it all and Tim would be arrested for burglary.

He had to find more evidence, and he had an idea where to start looking.

Aunt Josephine was in bed when Tim returned, but she spoke to him through her bedroom door, "Is that you, Timothy?"

"Yeah, it's me."

"Lock the door behind you, will you please?"

The front door had a deadbolt latch, and Tim shoved the bolt in place. He went to his bedroom, put the pilfered file folders on top of a chiffonier, undressed, and went to bed.

A chilly wind swept down on the city from the mountain range to the west. Fall was in the air, and Tim wished he'd borrowed his late uncle's jacket. The walk to the general hospital took nearly an hour, and he was glad he'd worn his old boots and old clothes.

Inside, he walked past a dozen sick-looking men and women in the lobby and approached a woman in a white cap sitting behind a desk.

"I'd like to see David Wight, please."

She was a plump, gray-haired woman, so accustomed to listening to complaints of the ill that she had long ago lost any good humor she might have had. Her shrewd eyes took in his appearance, and her mind catalogued him as a hoodlum, the same kind of man as David Wight. "Ward two, second floor. That way." She nodded to her right.

His boots made clumping sounds on the wooden floor of the corridor, but now, he realized with relief, he didn't have to be quiet. He found ward two just as a nurse carrying a covered pan left. It was a big room with nine beds, all filled with men. Hacking, coughing, groaning men. The room smelled of antiseptic, medicine, and sickness. It also smelled of urine. Another nurse carrying an empty bed pan came in.

"Pardon me, ma'am, can you point out David Wight to me?"

"There. By the window."

David Wight was lying on his left side with his eyes closed. He opened his eyes when he sensed someone standing beside his bed. He was middle-aged, needing a shave. His small, gray eyes showed no recognition.

"Do you know who I am?" Tim asked.

The head turned from side to side.

"My name is Timothy Higgins."

Recognition came then. David Wight's mouth opened and a groan and a grunt came out. "You, you're . . ." He turned onto his back.

"Supposed to be dead, huh? Well, I'm not." Tim's voice was hard. "And I'll tell you something else, I'm the man who shot you."

"Huh? What?" The voice was that of a sick man.

"Yeah, I was there in the house on Jewell Street."

The small eyes closed, opened, and squinted.

"But you won't tell the police, will you. Because you don't want the police to know anything about you.

225

Well, I know all about you."

The mouth opened. A front tooth was missing and the remainder were a dirty brown. "Uh, you, uh, you're the one?"

"Yeah."

"What, uh, why?"

"You know why. You helped steal a hundred and three head of cattle in Parker County. Make that a hundred and four, including the one you gave to a farmer. I know the cattle were sold at the Union Stockyards, and I know whose name is on the bill of sale. Benjamin Jones. He's dead, you know."

David Wight groaned and grunted. He made a weak effort to raise up in the bed, but gave up and fell back.

"You're gonna live. If you lived this long, you'll stay alive. But you're gonna spend a long time in jail. When I go to the police with what I know about you, you'll leave this hospital in leg irons."

"No . . . don't."

"Why shouldn't I?"

"Don't. I, uh . . ." The small eyes closed.

Tim squatted beside the bed and put his face closer. "I'll make a trade. You answer some questions for me and I'll forget I saw you."

The eyes opened. "What?"

"Who fixed up the records in the state government to make it look like Benjamin Jones owned four or five different cattle brands?"

"Don't know. He . . . he wouldn't say."

"Who bought the cattle."

"A, uh, man from the U.S. Government."

"Who? What's his name?"

David Wight swallowed again. "Feller's a Indian agent. Buys cattle and stuff for the reservations. Buys

226

stole cattle."

"Huh?" Tim recoiled as if he'd been slapped in the face. "You . . . you don't mean the U.S. Government?"

"Yeah."

"Uh . . ." Now Tim was stammering weakly. "An Indian agent? How . . . who?"

A sneer came to the lips of David Wight, and a weak hand reached for a glass of water on a bedside table. Tim handed him the water. The weak hand held it to his lips, and David Wight took two swallows. The sneer returned and the voice was stronger.

"You're just a kid. You don't know nothin'."

"An Indian agent buys stolen cattle?"

"Bought yours. Fifty cents on the dollar."

"Jaysus H. Christmas."

"You're just a ignorant kid."

It took a full minute for Tim to absorb that, then he asked, "Who? What's his name?"

A dry chuckle came out of David Wight. "Wouldn't you like to know."

"You'll tell me or you'll tell the police."

The man in the bed swallowed again. "You won't say anything about me to the laws if I tell you?"

"No. No, I won't."

"Is that a promise? You givin' me your word?"

"Yeah, that's a promise. I won't say anything about you to the police."

"Name's McCeogh."

"Huh?" Again, Tim was dumbfounded. "What? What did you say?"

David Wight managed to speak louder. "I said his name's McCeogh. Alfred McCeogh."

"Jaysus H. Christmas."

227

Chapter Twenty-six

It was a long walk to Mary Jane's house that night. He hadn't bothered to change into his new clothes. It wasn't a social call. Half his mind wanted to go back and write his dad a letter apologizing for not finding the stolen cattle. But the other half told him to do what he had to do, and directed his steps ahead. He paused on the path in front of the house, the big house, a rich man's house. It took him several moments to gather his nerve and go knock on the door. She answered his knock as he was afraid she would, and again she stepped outside and into his arms. Her kiss was warm and sweet and her body hugged his.

All he could do was swallow a lump in his throat.

"Is something wrong, Timothy?"

"Well, uh, Mary Jane, is your dad at home?"

"Why, yes. Why?"

"I have to see him. Business."

Her eyes studied his face in the dim light. He could feel her eyes. She said, "Something is the matter. What?"

"I have to talk with him."

She was impatient. "Will you tell me why?"

He wished he were somewhere else. He wished this whole mess had never happened. "I, uh, it's between me and him."

"Oh, it is, is it?" When he said nothing further, she added, "All right, come in."

Alfred McCeogh got up from his deep leather chair and put down the newspaper he was holding. "Why, it's Timothy Higgins, isn't it?" He held out his hand to shake.

Tim shook hands with him, but his grip was weak. "Mr. McCeogh, I have to talk with you. Alone."

A puzzled frown came over the older man's round face. "What's this all about?"

"Can we be alone, sir?"

"Well, all right. Come into my study." He led the way into another, smaller room, a room that held a desk, a wall of bookcases, a leather-covered desk chair, and an overstuffed easy chair. It had a big bay window that looked out on the street.

The older man closed the door, dropped into the desk chair, and repeated his question, "What's this all about?"

Tim didn't know how to say it. He had to say it. The words came out in a rush, "You bought a hundred and three head of beeves that were stolen from the HL Ranch, and you knew they were stolen."

Alfred McCeogh's mouth dropped open. His face turned white. For a long moment, he couldn't speak. Then, "You don't know what you're saying."

"Yes, sir, I do."

A mixture of disbelief, understanding, horror, and

229

then anger came over McCeogh's face. His features were pulled down tight. "You're talking bullshit. Pure bullshit."

For the first time since he'd left the hospital, a doubt crept into Tim's mind. Had David Wight lied? Did he know what he was talking about? He was a thief, a blackguard, a man who would say anything to save his own hide.

Tim's voice quavered, "Yes, sir, I, uh, I believe I do." But dammit, he hadn't come here without giving it a lot of thought. He couldn't back down now. He set his jaw and added, "You know damn well I know what I'm talking about. It can be proven. There are records. Most of the thieves are still alive and they'll tell all about it. One of them is in the general hospital right now. And you had to file false papers with the Bureau of Indian Affairs."

Alfred McCeogh jumped up. "Get out of this house."

Tim stood his ground. "You had a very profitable deal going. You bought cattle and groceries for the Indians, and overcharged the U.S. Government. You bought stolen cattle and paid only fifty cents on the dollar and charged the U.S. Government top dollar. You put the difference in the bank. I'll bet you even charged the government for things you didn't buy for the Indians. And up there in the mountains, you had to take a look at those cattle where they were being held at the railroad spur lines, at the old mine. You sent your daughter in another direction and told her where to meet you later. She got lost. You almost caused her death." It was a long speech, and Tim was out of breath.

The older man yelled, "Get out."

230

"Fine. I'll go. But you're going to hear from the U.S. marshals tomorrow." He put his hand on the doorknob. "And you can't stand an investigation."

"Wait." McCeogh's features had softened. His shoulders slumped as he sat in his desk chair again. "What . . . what do you want?"

Tim had been thinking about it and had reached a decision. "I want two things. I want the money for those cattle, every cent you charged the government, and I want you to resign. Your days of dealing with thieves and cheating the government are over."

Mary Jane's father was sick. Tim thought he was going to throw up. He looked at Tim with sick eyes. "What . . . what if I do that? Will you go to the federal marshals?"

"No. You're the dad of a girl I like a lot. I, un . . ." He was almost sick himself when he thought of Mary Jane. "For her sake, I won't say anything. But on those two conditions."

"All right. Agreed. I, uh, have the money here in my safe. Do you want it tonight?"

"Yeah."

"How much?"

"Five thousand two hundred dollars."

"Why that . . . that's impossible."

"That's the market price for one hundred and four head of prime beeves. That's what the rightful owner of the beeves is entitled to."

"But I only made a profit of half that much. You'll have to get the rest out of the men who stole the cattle."

Tim shook his head. "The thieves, most of them, are scattered, and I haven't got time to track them down. I got four hundred dollars from one, and that only partly

231

pays me for . . . everything. You'll have to cough up the full price."

"I haven't got that much."

"Yes, you have. That's what the U.S. Government paid."

"I'll, uh, I'll have to get you a check."

"All right. A cashier's check. Made out to my dad, John Higgins. Which bank?"

"The, uh, the First National."

"I'll meet you there at ten o'clock in the morning."

The older man still looked sick.

"Agreed?"

McCeogh only nodded his head.

"I'll let myself out. Ten o'clock. Be there."

Now came the part that he dreaded. Mary Jane met him as he came out of the room. "Timothy?" Worry frowns wrinkled her forehead. "What happened? I heard yelling."

"Yeah. Can I talk to you outside?"

She led the way to the door, and they went out onto the porch. She waited for him to speak.

"Mary Jane, you're going to hate me, and I don't blame you. Your dad and I had a falling out. A real bad falling out. Over business. I'm sorry." It was one of the few times he'd ever apologized to anyone. White Shirt Higgins believed apologies were a sign of weakness. "I'm really sorry."

She studied his face. "What happened?"

Shaking his head, he said, "I'd rather let him tell you."

"Does this mean that you and I are . . . are no longer friends?"

He blurted, "I wish it wasn't so, Mary Jane. I wish to

232

God it wasn't so."

Silence. Then, "After I talk to my father, can I see you again?"

"If you want to. You know where to find me. But . . . I don't think you'll want to."

Her face screwed up as if she was in pain, and she uttered, "Timothy, uh, oh my God." She turned, swiftly, and went inside.

It was an even longer walk back to Aunt Josephine's house. His feet dragged. He wasn't proud of himself. In fact, he felt guilty. He'd hurt the only girl he'd ever been close to. Her family would have to sell their big house and move, probably out of the city. Her father's government career was ruined. A hundred-year-old dying man couldn't have felt worse. Had he done the right thing?

"How the hell would I know," he mumbled. "I'm just a dumb, ignorant kid. Five years from now, or ten, I'll look back on this and then maybe I'll know.

"And maybe I'll never know."

With time to kill after breakfast, he addressed an envelope to John Higgins, HL Ranch, Shiprock, Colorado, and borrowed a postage stamp from his aunt. After a night of tossing and turning in his bed, he felt even older than he'd felt the night before, and Aunt Josephine commented, "You're awfully quiet lately, Timothy. Is anything the matter? Did you have a disagreement with that girl?"

"Yeah, I did."

She knew better than to ask about it.

When the time came, he stuffed the envelope in his shirt pocket, walked to East Colfax, and rode a streetcar to Seventeenth Street. He got to the First National Bank at two minutes until ten. Harold McCeogh wasn't inside, but when Tim stepped back outside he saw the older man coming. They met outside the bank door.

"Now see here," McCeogh said, "I've been thinking about this, and this just isn't right. I should not be held accountable for what someone else made in a cattle transaction."

With a negative shake of his head, Tim said, "That won't do. I want every cent those cattle were worth. Maybe you can get some of it back from the thieves."

McCeogh looked up and down the street, afraid they would be overheard. Pedestrians passed by but paid them no mind. "Why, this is . . . this is blackmail. Think of what this will do to my family."

"I've thought of that. I wish there was a way to keep from hurting them. But my dad is entitled to the full market price, and you're the only one who can pay."

McCeogh's round face was red with anger. "This is blackmail."

But Tim's face was getting red, too. Wouldn't you know this sonofabitch would try to use his daughter and wife to help him wiggle out of trouble. "We've talked enough, and I've seen all I want to see of you. Are you gonna pay up or not?"

For a moment, McCeogh appeared to be on the verge of fainting. Finally, he said weakly, "All right. Wait here."

Tim followed him into the bank and watched while

234

he went to a teller's window. It took fifteen minutes, and Tim stood on first one foot and then another. When McCeogh met him again, he handed him a cashier's check for five thousand and two hundred dollars. Tim took it, looked it over, and left without another word.

It was a four-block walk to the post office, and there Tim put the check in the envelope addressed to his dad and dropped it in a mail slot.

Now the score was settled. John White Shirt Higgins was paid for the stolen cattle, and Tim had four hundred dollars of a dead thief's money. It was done—almost.

He told his aunt some of what had happened, but not everything. He didn't tell her about killing a man and he didn't tell her about breaking two thieves out of jail. He told her only that he had found out what had happened to the cattle, who had sold them and who had bought them, and that he had been paid in full with a cashier's check, which he had just mailed to his dad. In anticipation of her questions, he explained that if he had turned the thieves over to the law he wouldn't have gotten the money, and he didn't think they would steal again.

Aunt Josephine didn't understand it all, but she said, "You're nearly a grown man, Timothy, and I'm sure you did what you think is best."

He sighed and his shoulders slumped. "I hope so, Aunt Josie. Lord, I hope so."

"Are you going to stay here and try to get your job back?"

"I don't know. I just don't know what to do."

"You've been terribly busy, Timothy, and you've

235

been through a lot of suffering. Why don't you just rest here a while and then decide what you want to do. You know you're welcome here."

He went to the water closet, took the bandage off his head, and noted with satisfaction that a hard scab had formed over the wound. In another week or two the hair would have the wound completely covered.

When the newspaper was thrown into the front yard by a boy on a bicycle, he brought it inside, scanned it hurriedly, and then looked through it carefully. There was no mention of a broken window at the state capitol building, and there was no mention of a break in at the Secretary of State's office. Somebody, for some reason, was keeping it quiet.

Tim put the paper down and stared at the floor.

He had one more chore to do.

Chapter Twenty-seven

Louis Rondeau himself came to the long counter when Tim stepped inside the state office. "What is it this time?" He sounded more impatient than anything else.

"What I want to say, Mr. Rondeau, had better be said in your private office."

Suspicion showed in the politician's eyes. He hooked his thumbs in his suspenders, and his heavy jowls nearly surrounded his stub of a cigar. "Is that so?"

"That's so." Tim looked beyond the man and saw a carpenter in his overalls repairing the splintered door jamb.

Rondeau shifted the cigar from one side of his mouth to the other and finally said, "All right, come in."

He turned and went into his office. Tim went around the long counter and followed. Clerical workers stared, and one of them, a short man with a pencil-thin moustache, started to follow Tim inside the office. He stopped when Rondeau turned and gave him a barely perceptible shake of the head.

"Now, what's this all about?" The politician plopped down in his desk chair. Tim remained standing.

"It's about some doctored brand books. Removable pages and brands registered to two different people. One of them Benjamin Jones."

"Oh, that," Rondeau shrugged as if nothing worried him. "It's like I said the other day, clerks do make mistakes."

"It's no mistake. I've got the proof."

Louis Rondeau leaned forward and put his elbows on the desk. He smiled. "How old are you, son?"

"What's that got to do with anything?"

"You're still wet behind the ears. You're imagining things."

Shaking his head, Tim said, "Huh-uh. Don't give me that. I'm the one who broke in here and took your files. The newspapers would get a kick out of seeing those files. I've read the *Rocky Mountain News* enough to know they like that kind of story."

The smile disappeared. The heavy jowls squared. "You broke in here? You're the one?"

Tim didn't answer, only met the older man's gaze head on.

"I can have you arrested. You're a burglar, a thief."

"Why don't you? You didn't even report the break in to the police. You don't want anybody asking questions. Like how a known criminal got his name opposite the brands of four honest ranchers. How much was Benjamin Jones paying you? Did he give you a percentage? Boy, the newspaper is going to like this."

The politician jumped up so fast he knocked his chair over. He opened his mouth to yell, then changed his mind. Slowly, he picked up the chair and sat in it.

"You're a pretty smart kid. How come you haven't already gone to the newspapers or the police?"

Tim had hoped to keep the answer to that question to himself, but now he decided to be frank. "Because I don't want to stick around here. I don't want to get mixed up in any legal horseshit. I've got other things to do."

"Uh-huh." Rondeau considered that. "So what do you want?"

"Your resignation. Today."

"Hmm." The older man leaned back in his chair, appearing to be completely at ease. "Where are my files?"

"Where you won't find them."

"Where are you staying? At a hotel?"

A warning suddenly tugged at Tim's mind, and he decided to lie. "Yeah."

"All right. If you'll bring me back my files, I'll tender my resignation."

"No. You resign and I'll burn the files."

Rondeau shrugged. "You win. I'll have my resignation on the governor's desk within the hour."

It was easy, too easy, and for a moment, Tim could only stare in disbelief.

"Isn't that what you want?"

"Yeah."

"And you'll destroy those papers?"

"Uh, yeah. As soon as I read in the newspapers that you resigned."

"It'll be in tomorrow's papers."

There was no more to be said. Tim turned to go. "I'll be watching."

*   *   *

Outside, the sky was threatening rain, or possibly snow, and Tim turned up his shirt collar and shivered in the cool air. It was too easy. Something didn't fit. Sure, Benjamin Jones was dead, and his death ended any deal he had worked out with the Secretary of State. That profitable arrangement was over. But Louis Rondeau still wouldn't give up his elected job so easy. It cost money to campaign for election. Money and a lot of smooth talking. Rondeau was a smooth talker. He'd try to talk his way out.

The warning that had tugged at Tim's mind was back. He glanced behind him, and the warning tugged harder.

He was being followed.

It was one of the clerks in Rondeau's office, the short man with the thin moustache. He was wearing a fedora hat now and a coat over his vest. At first, Tim wasn't sure, but when he turned a corner and looked back, the short man was still behind him. Tim's steps quickened, but on second thought, he slowed down. No use running a foot race. What the man wanted wasn't hard to figure out. He wanted to know where Tim was staying and where he was keeping those files.

Realizing that, Tim turned another corner and headed away from his aunt's house. The short man kept his position. Tim walked a block, turned another corner and went back to East Colfax, back to the streetcars and pedestrians. The short man walked faster and was gaining.

He knows now, Tim thought. He knows I'm wise to him and I'm not going to lead him anywhere. He ought to give up and go back. But the man was still gaining.

That warning tug came again.

Tim looked back in time to see the man reach inside his coat and pull out a short-barreled revolver.

Cold fear knifed through Tim's stomach and sent a chill into his throat. "Oh no," he groaned.

The gun popped at the same instant Tim threw himself aside, against the wall of a brick building. The explosion drowned out the sound of a clanging streetcar and stopped pedestrians in their tracks.

Tim's left arm went numb, and he was knocked back so hard he fell onto the seat of his pants. A woman screamed a high, thin scream. A man yelled. Footsteps hurried toward him. Stopped. "Hey," someone yelled.

But the people stayed back. Stayed back and watched helplessly, as the short man came close, the gun still in his hand. Though his voice was silent, Tim's mind screamed, too.

Do something, somebody.

But he knew they could do nothing. On the frontier, men were armed, and they wouldn't just watch a cold-blooded murder happen. Not so in the civilized city. Only the police and hoodlums were armed, and there were more hoodlums than police.

The man was sure of himself. He had the only weapon. He walked close enough that he couldn't miss with the snub-nosed gun.

Tim's mind screamed again. Do something yourself. Don't just sit here. What? It came to him in a flash— how old Spook had once stampeded when he saw Tim's hat sailing toward him.

In another flash, Tim grabbed his hat by the brim and sailed it at the gunman. The gun boomed again, but the slug smashed into the brick wall as Tim's hat hit the gunman in the face.

In another quick move, Tim was on his feet, and in three steps he was ramming his head into the gunman's stomach.

The short man went down with Tim on his knees on top of him. Tim's knees pounded him in the stomach and in the crotch, and Tim's right hand groped for the gun. His teeth were bared in a desperate grimace as he got hold of the gun and tried to twist it out of the short man's hand. His left arm dangled helplessly.

The gunman got hold of Tim's hair with his left hand, pulled back, bucked and twisted, and was winning the struggle.

Suddenly it was over.

A pedestrian, a husky man in baggy wool pants and heavy jackboots, planted one of his boots on the gunman's right wrist, pinning it to the brick pavement. He reached down and easily took the gun out of the gunman's hand.

"Stay right there, mister." His voice held a deadly warning.

Slowly, Tim got to his feet. His left shirtsleeve was bloody above the elbow, and his left arm was lifeless. The sight of the bloody arm almost made him sick to his stomach. The gunman stayed down, flat on his back, as people gathered around.

"We'd better get you to a hospital, young feller," the husky one said. "Anybody got a carriage?"

"I have," a voice answered. "Right down the street. I'll get it."

"Wait a minute." Tim tried to fight down the bile in his throat. He looked down at the gunman. "I know who sent you, but I want you to tell everybody here." He summoned some strength and yelled, "Name him."

A sneer spread over the gunman's face, but not

for long.

"Name him, mister." The husky one raised his foot and held it over the prone man's face. The foot in its jackboot had to be at least a size fourteen. "We all saw what happened, and you better talk or your brains are gonna be spread all over these bricks."

The sneer turned to cold fear. "It was Rondeau. He told me to."

"Who?"

"Louis Rondeau. I'm only carrying out his orders."

Turning to the crowd, Tim said, "You all heard that?"

"Yes," a man's voice answered. "The police are coming."

"You need a doctor, young man. My carriage is right here."

He felt no pain, only a numbness in his left arm, and he walked into the hospital. He was immediately led to a bed, and his shirt was cut off.

"Your name?"

"Timothy Higgins."

"Who is your next of kin?" The woman wore a white dress and a white cap.

"Am I that bad off?"

"No. Just routine. A doctor will be here soon."

He gave his Aunt Josephine's name and address. "But for Pete's sake, tell her I'm not going to die, will you. She'll die herself with worry."

He was pushed down, and a mask was put over his face. It had a strong odor he didn't recognize, something like the lineament the HL used on horses. The ceiling swam and slowly dissolved.

243

Chapter Twenty-eight

The first face he saw was a man's. A smooth-shaven face with thick brown hair parted in the middle. The face was looking at him intently, studying his face. It spoke:

"I'm Dr. Malcom. Can you hear me?"

He mumbled, "Yes, sir. How's my arm?" He looked down at himself. A white sheet covered him up to his chin. He tried to move his arms. The left one wouldn't move.

"No, your left arm is immobile, and it will be for some time. But you're fortunate. Here's the situation. Your left arm has a puncture wound through the, uh, bicep muscles. The bone was broken about halfway between your elbow and your shoulder."

Hopefully, "It's gonna heal, though, huh?"

"Yes, it will heal, and you will have the use of it. But," the young doctor shook his head sadly, "it will always be a little crooked."

"Crooked?" Tim tried to raise up in the bed. "I'm gonna have a crooked arm?"

"Now don't try to move. It could be much worse. Yes, it will be a little crooked, and it will never be as strong as your right arm, but it will heal and you will be able to use it."

Tim sank back in the bed. A gloomy fog settled over him. "Oh, boy."

The next face he saw was Aunt Josephine's. She sat in a chair beside his bed, and there were tears on her face. When she saw his eyes open she forced herself to smile.

"You're awake, Timothy. Welcome back to the world."

"Yeah, I'm awake. The doctor said I'm gonna have a crooked arm."

"Yes. But Timothy," she was trying her best to be cheerful, "think of how lucky you are. You've been shot twice now, and you're still alive and in one piece."

He forced himself to grin. "Yeah, when you think of it that way, you're right. I'm really pretty lucky."

"And the doctor said you'll be able to use your left arm. It just won't be quite as strong."

"Good thing I'm not a southpaw." He raised up on the bed, pushed the sheet down and looked at his arm. It was bent at the elbow and covered with plaster of paris from his shoulder down to his wrist. "When can I get out of here?"

"Tomorrow, probably. The doctor wants you to stay in bed another day."

"I don't see why."

"Doctor's orders, Timothy. Please do as he says."

Grinning at her concern, he said, "For your sake, Aunt Josie, I'll do it."

She was silent, looking down at her high-top button

shoes. She spoke again without looking up. "Timothy, I did something that I probably shouldn't have."

"Naw. Not you."

"When they came and told me you were in the hospital I came right over and saw you were asleep and I didn't want to wake you up, so I went to see Mary Jane McCeogh. I thought she'd want to know, and I thought you'd want her to know."

"What did she say?"

Aunt Josephine looked at him. "She said—I wish I hadn't gone—she said you are no longer friends. I'm sorry, Timothy. I hope you're not mad at me."

A long sigh came from him and he shook his head sadly. When he looked at his aunt, he saw she was on the verge of tears. He forced another smile.

"Aunt Josie, there is nothing—nothing in the world—you could do to make me mad at you."

The next face he saw was middle-aged, with a thick soup-strainer moustache and a hawk nose. It was looking down at him.

"You're Timothy Higgins?"

He had an air of authority, and a worry crept into Tim's mind. How much did he know? "Yeah, that's my name."

"I'm detective Johnson of the Denver police. The doctor tells me you're well enough to talk." He sat in the bedside chair.

"Sure."

"Tell me what happened."

"I was shot."

"We know that. We took statements from witnesses

at the scene. What we don't know is why."

"I had an argument with the Secretary of State."

"Uh-huh. What did you argue about?"

There was no way out of it. Tim had hoped to avoid any contact with the police, and he sure didn't want to be a witness at a trial. But he couldn't lie. He told the detective about the altered brand records, how a man named Benjamin Jones was able to sell somebody else's cattle because of the altered records. He told how a hundred and three head of his dad's cattle had been stolen and sold by Benjamin Jones. He didn't mention Alfred McCeogh.

"Benjamin Jones. I've heard that name recently."

"I read in the newspapers that he was shot in a house on Jewell Street."

"Oh, him. How did you know about these brand records?"

He told how he had become suspicious and had broken into the Secretary of State's office.

"You broke in? I didn't hear about a break in."

"I've got the papers. I can show them to you."

"Where are they?"

"At my aunt's house. In my bedroom. She'll find them for you." He gave the detective his aunt's address.

The detective stood. "We're getting a warrant for the arrest of Louis Rondeau. We'll be back to talk to you." He left.

They made a neat white sling for his arm, and he was happy to discover that his fingers worked. Aunt Josephine met him at her door, welcomed him with a kiss on the cheek, and told him about the detectives coming to get the papers he had in his bedroom.

"Now I want you to just rest, Timothy. I don't want you to go right back to doing things the way you did the first time you were shot."

His spirits were low. "If they arrested that Louis Rondeau and are gonna bring him to trial, I'll have to stick around whether I want to or not. I'd try to find a job, but who'd hire a man with one arm." He dropped into a living room chair and sat there, head down.

Try as he would, he couldn't help thinking about her. She didn't want to see him. They were no longer friends. He didn't blame her, but he couldn't help thinking about her.

Then the mailman came and brought him a letter.

"Dear Son," he read. "I hope this letter catches up with you. I sent Stub to try to find you, and he found out you'd been shot and patched up by a doctor in Rosebud, but he lost the trail there. If you get this please come home. I am dying. Your dad."

He reread the letter three times and handed it to his aunt, who read it twice.

"Oh, Timothy, you certainly have your troubles."

"I've got to go. Trial or no trial."

"I'm sure they would understand."

He stood wearily, feeling awkward with his left arm in a sling. "I'll go buy a ticket and find out when the train leaves."

The best route, he was told at the Union Station, was the Denver and Rio Grande to Pueblo, then west. The train pulled out at eight o'clock in the morning.

At his aunt's house again, he borrowed one of his late uncle's valises and packed his old boots and old denim pants. He wore his new boots and new gabardines. Still

248

feeling low, he slouched around the house. Aunt Josephine tried to cheer him up.

"Maybe he isn't dying, Timothy. Once before when you were here he wrote and said he was sick, and when you got home you found he was just as strong as ever."

"Yeah, you never know what to expect. But I've got to go."

It was the evening newspaper that gave him something else to think about—for a little while. A banner headline screamed:

SECRETARY OF STATE A SUICIDE

"Oh, no," Tim groaned.

The story told about Louis Rondeau's arrest on the charge of being an accessory to attempted murder. It told about the politician's using his belt and shoelaces to hang himself by the neck in his jail cell. The story went on and on, but Tim read no further.

He showed the newspaper to his aunt. "Well, that ends it."

Aunt Josephine read every word, then said, "Did you read this part, about the man who shot you? He admitted it all."

"He did? Good. There won't be a trial, then."

"It really is over, isn't it, Timothy."

"Yeah. Except that . . . I wonder what's going on at the HL."

It took two days to get to Gunnison on the western slope of Colorado. The train went through some of the most scenic mountain country in the world. The aspens were all yellow now and aspen leaves were falling like flakes of gold. They looked like gold coins on the ground. The buckbrush had turned red, and the wild geraniums were every color in the rainbow. High peaks off in the distance were white with snow.

Tim was glad to get out of the city and into the open country. He knew now, without doubt, that he wasn't cut out to be a city dweller. He needed elbow room, breathing room, and he needed good horses, and cowboys to associate with, men who talked his language.

But unhappy thoughts kept running through his mind. He had killed a man. He had caused another man to kill himself, and he had ruined still another man's career. He had blackmailed that man.

And he had lost her.

Repeatedly, he reminded himself that it was over now. Everything had ended. But he felt a heavy weight in his chest.

At Gunnison he had breakfast in a workingman's cafe and boarded a stage to Shiprock, a four-hour ride. The coach bounced and swayed on its leather thoroughbraces, and Tim and the other passengers were thrown from one side to the other. Three times, the stage stopped to change horses, and tired four-up teams were led away to be watered and fed while fresh teams were hitched to the singletrees.

Finally, the stage pulled up with a loud "Whoa" and a rattling of trace chains, and the passengers stepped out in front of Shiprock's three-story clapboard hotel.

Tim had no more than stepped onto the plank sidewalk when he was met by a man with a badge pinned to his vest. But Sheriff Windecker held out his hand to shake.

"I knew you'd be coming back, Tim, and I was keeping an eye out for the stage. I'm afraid I've got bad news for you, son."

Tim could guess what the news was, and he said "Can we talk in your office?"

"Shore, Tim."

Neither man spoke until they got there. They sat, and the sheriff pushed back his broad-brimmed hat and started rolling a cigarette. He eyed the cast on Tim's left arm, and the sling, but asked no questions. The office held a scarred rolltop desk and three wooden chairs. A gunrack on one wall held two lever action rifles and a double-barreled shotgun. Another wall was almost covered with wanted posters. The town's one-cell jail was empty.

"My dad is dead." Tim said it with resignation.

"Yeah, Tim. We buried him yesterday on that little hill back of the HL house, where your mother is buried."

"What killed him?"

"Cancer. The same thing that killed his dad, your granddad. He had it in his guts, and it ate on him for a long time. He knew it was going to kill him. He'd known it for a year or more."

"He didn't say."

"He wouldn't."

They were silent a moment, and Tim's mind told him: This is something else that has ended.

Then the sheriff shifted in his chair and opened a desk drawer. "He wrote you a letter and asked me to give it to you if you didn't get back before he died."

Tim took the envelope and hesitated. He wanted to

251

be alone when he opened it, but he had no place to go. The lawman read his mind, and stood.

"I got to go see about something, Tim. You just set here as long as you want to." He strode out the door.

It was a short letter: "Dear son. I got the check for the cattle today and put it in the bank. I know how much backbone and bulldog stubbornness it took for you to get this check. I'm proud of you. The HL is yours now, and I'm departing this world knowing I couldn't leave it in better hands. Your dad."

He felt no anguish, no sorrow. Maybe he would later, but not now. Now he only felt sad. Weary. Like a hundred-year-old man.

He refolded the letter slowly, thoughtfully, holding it to his left side and using the fingers of his left hand. He put it back in the envelope and stuffed it in his shirt pocket. Outside, he tried to think of a way to get to the HL headquarters. He needed a horse. Sheriff Windecker solved that problem. He had been waiting outside.

"Expect you'll be wanting to go home, Tim. Take one of my horses. Tell old Scrubby at the livery barn I said to give you my sorrel mare."

"Thanks. I'll bring her back."

"Whenever you feel like it, Tim." The sheriff went into his office.

Tim turned his steps toward the livery four blocks away, beyond the end of the sidewalk. He heard his name called. A soft voice, feminine.

At first, when he stopped and looked back, he didn't recognize her. She wore a long dress with a white lacy collar and cuffs, a dress with a belt that pulled it in at the waist, showing a figure that was slender but very much female. Her light brown hair was parted neatly

252

on the side and held in place by a red ribbon.

Then he recognized her short nose, straight mouth, and firm chin.

"Ellen. I'm glad to see you made it back."

"Hello, Timothy. Yes, we got back with no trouble. I delivered your horses and saddles to Stub at the HL. They're fine."

"How is old Joe?"

She smiled. Her teeth were not perfect, but they were white. A nice smile. "He's a believer now, Timothy. He's your friend for life. He and my mother are living on the homestead."

"I was kind of worried about you two. They were looking for a man and woman on horseback. I guess they don't know anything about that around here, though."

"No. That's all behind us." Another smile lit up her face. "I'm an honest woman now. I even got a job in the bank. I'm living in town."

The smile slipped and her forehead wrinkled. "I'm sorry about Mr. Higgins."

"Yeah."

"He was a hard man and I know he was hard on you, but I think he wanted you to prove yourself." A half smile returned. "And, boy, did you ever."

"Huh." Tim snorted. "Yeah."

Her eyes went to his left arm held in the white sling. "I would very much like to hear about what happened in Denver after we left. I know you want to get back to the ranch and you have a lot of things to do, but maybe sometime . . ." She left the rest unsaid.

"Sure. And I'd like to hear about what happened to you."

"Maybe I could fix you some supper when you're in town, when you feel like it, and we could talk."

"That sounds like a good idea. We've got things to talk about. In fact, that's a very good idea."

She turned to go. "Well, I have to get back to work. Until then, good-bye, Tim."

He watched her walk away, back straight, head up. A pretty girl. Watched her until she went into the bank building a block away, out of sight.

A small smile turned up the corners of his mouth. A lot of things had ended. A lot of things were over.

Now maybe—just maybe—something good was about to begin.

WHITE SQUAW
Zebra's Adult Western Series
by E. J. Hunter